Beautiful Girl Thumb

Beautiful Girl Thumb

and other stories

Melissa Steele

TURNSTONE PRESS

Turnstone Press
Artspace Building
018-100 Arthur Street
Winnipeg, MB
R3B 1H3 Canada
www.TurnstonePress.com

Turnstone Press gratefully acknowledges the assistance of the Canada Council for the Arts, the Manitoba Arts Council, the Government of Canada through the Book Publishing Industry Development Program, and the Government of Manitoba through the Department of Culture, Heritage and Tourism, Arts Branch, for our publishing activities.

Cover design: Doowah Design
Interior design: Sharon Caseburg
Printed and bound in Canada by Friesens for Turnstone Press.
Second printing: March 2007

Library and Archives Canada Cataloguing in Publication

Steele, Melissa, 1963-

Beautiful girl thumb : and other stories / Melissa Steele.

ISBN-13: 978-0-88801-318-7
ISBN-10: 0-88801-318-3

I. Title.

PS8587.T342B42 2006   C813'.54   C2006-905899-7

*for Sam, Rachel and Thomas
and for George, of course, because everything is*

Contents

Beautiful Girl Thumb

Beautiful Girl Thumb

Brianna stretches out in her attic room, her cellphone grafted to her perfectly shaped ear. Clothes, makeup, books and gum wrappers surround her. Postcards and cereal bowls, some decorated with dried milk and crusted Cheerios, dot the brown berber carpet. The walls slant dangerously. They are covered in posters of beautiful people—Marilyn, Rita, the Red Hot Chili Peppers with socks on their dongs, Sailor Moon and a life-size (well, for her) reclining version of Kate Moss that runs along the straight bit of wall on the north side. This attic is Brianna's space; sometimes she spends whole days without leaving it except to go downstairs and take a shower. Her stepmom and Kyle and Conrad (her two little half-brothers) act like they own the rest of the house and she doesn't want to compete with them for it.

It is Friday night. Brianna is wearing plaid boy's boxers and a tankini—lounging clothes. She is long and thin and gorgeous—

like the real Kate Moss, but there isn't a real Kate Moss, but if there were, she would look like Brianna. Bri has been a model, an actress, a writer, a born-again Christian and an environmental activist, and she is only nineteen. She has just put the finishing touches on her essay on *Twelfth Night* and Leonard Cohen's *Beautiful Losers*. It is the middle of the night but there is still time to find something fun to do. There is a rave her friend Delia invited her to, but she's not really into that any more. Delia's too desperate anyway. Maybe Jesse knows about a house party. Grapes wants to go out to the lake and skinny-dip in the dark. Really she'd like to do something with Teresa, just hang out at the Sals and order veggie nips and milkshakes and make fun of Teresa's gap-toothed boyfriend. That would be great if Teresa weren't such a back-stabbing *byotch* and wasn't always all over Jesse. She's just jealous, everyone says, but it doesn't make it hurt less. Maybe she should get Jesse to drive her out to the Assiniboine forest and they could swallow a whole lot of something potent and curl up together in the brush and never have to wake up again. That would be cool, but she's not a user anymore so she'll probably just stay home, locked in her garret like the Spirit of Christmas Past.

In the background, she's playing the Pixies on the CD player—"Monkey's gone to Heaven" is a song she loves because every word of it is true. Brianna revises her essay while she's on the phone with her mother, Alice, who lives in Taber, Alberta. Alice made spoiling Brianna her life's work. Then she married Danny, a retired bouncer with two mysteriously absent thumbs and an assertive stutter. After her mother's wedding, Brianna lived on strawberry licorice and E and made a point of pride of never leaving her basement room during daylight, no matter what the school had to say about it.

Alice and Danny threatened to kick Brianna out when she was sixteen because she was hanging out with users and was so drugged-up herself that her eyes, always large and round and awestruck, had become like two spinning discs. Her druggie friends called her Krazy Kat Moss and it suited her. Maybe they were being mean. Whatever.

When Brianna was expelled from school for carving Kurt Cobain's name on every desk in the geography classroom, Danny drove her to Calgary and put her on a plane to Winnipeg with nothing but two suitcases, one full of clothes, makeup and a pound of safety pins, and one full of stuffed animals, mostly pink terry cloth teddy bears. It was one part desperation on Alice's part, one part giving Brianna a fresh start and one part payback for Brianna's father, who thought he could just dump her and move on, no questions asked.

In Winnipeg, Brianna moved in with her egomaniacally helpless dad and her psycho/control freak stepmother and her twin three-year-old half-brothers. All on her own, she turned her life around, stopped using, started eating and became an honour student. At the moment Brianna is living clean and her only addiction is her cellphone—a make-up gift from Alice and her way of not losing Bri altogether. Brianna talks all the time on it, sometimes has people waiting on two or three lines, sometimes talks in the bath, or while doing ab crunches, or while putting away a box of Twinkies. Sometimes she falls asleep on the phone and wakes up to continue the conversation. Her mom is more or less a last resort.

"Mom, I hate my life." Brianna says this a lot. Her mother doesn't know what it means this time. (You ruined me. I'm bored. I'm hungry. I'm at this very moment swallowing a vast quantity of pharmaceuticals. All of the above.)

"Honey, it's so great to hear your voice. I love you, Sweetie.

Don't be sad, Snookim-Mookim. Don't cry. You're messing up your makeup. Shah. Shah."

"Mom, I don't think I can stand it any more. I've got these three exams and two essays and they signed me on for extra shifts at Patticakes. I wanna run a razor blade up and down my arm. I hate my goddamn useless fucking life." Brianna bangs down the phone on the carpet for emphasis.

"You tell that boy, Jesse, you're the best there is. You tell Jesse you deserve the best. You tell him, I want him to buy you Laura Secord chocolates and a silk nightie for Christmas. Jesse is a sweet boy, but don't let him think he can have it for free."

"Mom, do you have any idea who I even am?"

"You know, slipcase. Love crunches. Jubie jubes. You're worth your weight in gold, Sweetie, and you really should eat more. Do you think you're eating enough? Carrots are num— are you eating carrots? Danny can still check you into the clinic up here. Just for a few weeks, Honey. Just over the holidays. And I'll visit you every day and we'll do girl stuff and go shopping and play cards. It'll be so much fun, Brianna-Bandana. And then you'll be well."

"Mom, I'm not a freaking anorexic. I just ate a lot of licorice at one time. I'm not your little Swee' Pea princess any more. I'm an A student. I'm graduating. I'm not some screwed-up teenager any more. Why do you have to be so negative about me? I call you because I'm feeling lousy, and you just wanna check me into some fancy psych ward." While she talks, Brianna is spell-checking her essay and braiding and unbraiding her hair. At one point she has fifteen braids. Then none. Then a ballerina bun. Then Lily Tomlin ponytails.

"Now, Honey, it's just that Danny and I have talked about it and we love you and we want you back. Your dad doesn't understand about this stuff. He's so busy with his new wife and the twins. He just doesn't have time to take good care of you. And anyway, he's not a nurturer. He can't help it. He's just that way. He loves you, Honey, even if it seems like he's always thinking about something else. He loves you, he just can't show it. You know—men—" Mom's voice breaks into schoolgirl giggles and Brianna joins in half-heartedly.

"I know, Momsie. Anyway, I'm fine. I just turn around three times and disappear. It's easy." Brianna presses *Print* on her screen and jumps up and pirouettes across the room, the phone still glued to her ear. Her ponytails fly straight out from her head. "I'm just like a boarder here. I'm like one of Danny's missing thumbs—all healed but no hand to graft on to. I'm just this throbbing, beautiful girl thumb."

"Danny and I are your family, Sweetie. Come home."

"Thanks, Momsie-Whomsie. I know. My other line is going, Mom. Call me back later."

"It's already two in the morning here."

"Fine, then, don't call me back. Whatever. I gotta go."

"I love you, Snookim-Mookim."

"I love you, Momazoid."

Mom makes an *mmmm mmmm mmmm mmmm* sound until well after Brianna clicks over to the other line.

"Hey, Baby. It's me, Jesse."

"Jesse!"

"Hey, how's it gow'n?"

"How's it gow'n'?"

"How's it gow'n?"

"How's it gow'n with you, Pucky Do?"

"I just finished my mural," Jesse says. "It looks so fuckin' awesome. Do you wanna come over to my place and see it?"

"Maybeeeeee, Pucky Doodle Do," Brianna is getting

dressed. She is putting on a flowing black crepe skirt and a lime green ribbed sleeveless t-shirt.

"It's you and me. I did the whole back wall and the ceiling. It's totally us—true love forever—and some hearts and lady-bugs and a hookah—it's so cool."

"Chill, Jesse. My mom thinks you're getting too serious about me. I'm just an old throwaway thumb."

"How can I be too serious about the girl I'm going to marry?"

"I'm not the girl you're going to marry, Jesse-Bessee-Swee-tum-Do. It'll never work." Brianna decides the skirt is too frilly. She takes it off and tries out her orange stretch mini. Perfect. Her legs are practically gleaming.

"It'll work. We'll make it work, Baby."

"No, Jesse. You're great, but you're boring and your jokes are lame. You never say anything hardly. Anyway, your dick is too big. How can we get married if we can never do it without you hurting me?"

"I can change, Brianna-banana. I'll be whatever you want me to be. Whatever you say, Baby, I'm yours. I love you, Baby."

That word *Baby* the way boys say it to girls is so cloying. It reminds Brianna of what it tastes like to throw up a whole bag of red licorice. "Yeah, I love you too," she says. "It's just I feel like total shit. I'm going to flunk school and it's almost fucking Christmas. Hold on, there's my other line."

There is a *click* and Jesse is lost to her.

"Hey."

"Heey!"

"Heeeyyyyyy!!"

"Hee, hee, hee, what is this, some kind of pervert call?"

"Brianna, it's me. Garth."

"Hey, Grapes. How's it gow'n?"

"Good, can I come over? I got a hold of the new Tarantino script."

"Well, yeah, but Jesse wants me to come over to his place and see the mural he painted of me in his bedroom. Just one sec, Grapes." Brianna tosses the phone on the bed so she can slip off the green shirt and exchange it for one almost the same, but white with a little pink rose in the centre of the chest.

"When are you going to unload that greasy little creep?"

"I tried tonight. I told him his dick was so massive we could never have sex again. He doesn't get it."

"How can someone so stupid be so hard to get rid of?"

"You sound jealous, Grapes."

"Of course I'm jealous. The thought of you and Jesse together makes me writhe. You know you were made to be with me, Brianna. Why do you keep fighting it?"

"Uh, because your dick's so small? Just kidding, Grapes. You know you love it anyway."

"Hurt me. Hurt me."

"Anyway, Jesse's a nice guy. He's got a tattoo of me on his thigh. He would never cheat on me and he really loves me. I'd break up with him, but I can't stand to hurt him. I just wish he'd do something rotten sometime so that I wouldn't have to feel so damned mean. I'm suffocating."

"Use your imagination. He's probably doing it right now."

"He's not. He'd never."

"What makes you so sure?"

"I just remembered. He's still waiting on the other line. Hold on, Grapes."

"Yeah, later," Grapes says into the absolute sound of *click*.

"Baby?"

"Jesse?"

"It's me. Momsie. And Danny's here too. We just want you to eat something, Sugar."

Brianna grabs a Twinkie from one of several boxes on her night stand and stuffs half of it into her mouth. "Hear that? Is that the mouth of an anorexic psych case? Can you two lay off now, please?"

"You're not doing the puking thing are you, Sugar? You know how yellow that makes your teeth. Are you keeping anything down, Pookie?"

"Oh my God. If I am crazy I get it all from you. Wait. Just a sec."

There is that click again.

"Yo, yo, yo."

"It's me, Grapes. I'm outside in this amazing convertible red Dodge Prelude. Wanna go for a ride to Gimli? We can read the Tarantino script out loud and watch the sunrise."

"God, it's sweet that you try so hard, Grapes. Whose car is it? Oh, just a sec. I'm getting a beep."

"Yello," says Brianna, wiping her face and going over to look out the window to see Grapes in his brother's fancy car.

"Grapes, I said, I'll be right down. I just have to get dressed."

"No, it's me, Jesse."

"Jesse-Bessie-Boo! I love you so much, Jesse-Wessie. Your nose is so cute with those little nose hairs peeking out. Shoowheee. Shooowheeee."

"You coming over to see my mural? I'll pick you up."

"Wait, there's the other line again."

And that click again.

"It's Momsie again, Snippet. I've got Danny on the extension."

"Hi, Pookie," says Danny, sounding like a trained seal. "Your mother and I want you home. You must eat a healthy meal. You must get help."

"Mom, call off the narc. Why are you letting that thumbless ape talk for you?"

Then Alice's shaky, teary voice: "We'll tube feed you if we have to. I'm not letting you die just because your father's absent-minded."

"I'm getting a beep."

"Jesse?"

"No, it's Grapes. I've only got the car until eight o'clock tomorrow morning. Are you coming or what?"

Brianna heads over to the window. Outside the house is Grapes with his ear to his cellphone, idling in his brother's Dodge Prelude. Behind him, Jesse drives up in his mom's station wagon. It's funny watching him try to parallel park the thing.

"Grapes, go and talk to Jesse. He doesn't have a cell. Tell him I'm just getting dressed and I'll be right down."

"Are you coming to Gimli with me?"

"I'm not sure yet. Just give me five and I'll be down."

Brianna takes off the skirt and top and puts on her patchwork jeans and a white stretch tank that shows off her navel ring. She adds Jesse's jean jacket. She puts on platform sandals and decides to go with the ponytails. The make-up, just foundation, blush, lip gloss and mascara, only takes a few minutes. She grabs the essay from the printer and checks that all the pages are in order. She puts a paperclip on it and stuffs it into her school knapsack.

On the way down the stairs, Brianna runs smack into Kyle or Conrad, one of the twins. It is 4:30—they must be getting up for the day. As soon as one wakes up, he wakes the other

11

one up. Kyle or Conrad is carrying a plastic green cup and when he makes contact with his sister, the contents spill everywhere. It turns out the cup was full of toilet water and a perfectly round turd created by either Kyle or Conrad and scooped by one of them to prove to the other that he could and did make such a geometrically perfect object. The turd itself hits Brianna's jeans and slides down to rest on her sandal. Kyle and Conrad shriek with horror or delight and run into their room and lock the door. Brianna screams, "You little cretins," and kicks their door with her contaminated shoe. Most of the turd is flung onto the door where gravity takes over and it slides down to the floor, leaving a brown streak that resembles only itself—an unspeakably realistic smear of human feces.

Alexa, the stepmom, is there in the hallway looking like Judgment Day in a paisley flannel nightgown. "What's going on here?" she says to Brianna, as if whatever is going on must be Brianna's fault.

"Your little brats poured shit all over me and ran away laughing. Is that somehow my fault too?" Brianna says.

"There's two sides to every story," Alexa says, though in this case even she knows there isn't, couldn't be, a reasonable explanation.

Brianna's cellphone is ringing.

From the bedroom across the hall, Brianna's dad shouts out, "Who do I have to bump off to get a decent night's sleep around here?"

Brianna clicks the phone on and yells into it: "I'm living in a fucking horror movie."

Alexa points accusingly at the twins' door. This is code for *be a good example. Don't swear around your adorable little brothers,* but the guilt trip is lost on Brianna, who is already in the bathroom, extricating herself from her clothes and running a shower.

On the phone, Alice is saying, "We're leaving right now. We'll be there by tomorrow afternoon," but Brianna is in the shower feeling the warm, relaxing torrents of hard water on her body and can't hear anyone.

The Wedding Guest

Wednesday morning, the week of her wedding, Maureen met me at the Koffee Klutch, the little breakfast place we went to on Saturday mornings when we were living together six months ago now. I knew it was slightly humiliating to be meeting Maureen, my first and only crazy love, the woman for whom I had said I might like to be a father one day, the woman for whom I had agreed to drop out of graduate school and go through two years of education college hell so I would be in a position to support our hypothetical family, the woman who had dumped me for my physiotherapist, balding, steady Bob. It was humiliating that we were there, humiliating and ironic and maybe stupid, but I had argued to myself that it might also be the beginning of a literary event. I am a poet, so I am in the habit of consoling myself with the idea of my potential poems.

But I digress. I was telling you about breakfast. Maureen

and I were having our coffee. I had ordered eggs Benedict and Maureen had ordered French toast from the same red-haired, absent-looking waitress who had served us through countless Saturday mornings of tentative, but nevertheless love-like, passion. These Saturdays somewhere had dissolved into small irritations and larger ones and climaxed in endless plain old-fashioned bickering with a not-so-subtle undercurrent of rage. The last time we'd had breakfast at the Koffee Klutch, Maureen had used the occasion to announce that she was leaving me for Bob.

"Excuse me?"

"Bob. Your physiotherapist. I know this is hard, but I wanted to be honest and this is my life, you know. You're a nice guy, Kevin, and I'm sure you'll find someone who can be happy with you, but it's just not enough for me."

Bob. Happy. Nice. It's not enough. I had tried to process these words on the spot, right there while I was chewing a mouthful of eggs Benedict and English muffin. "Okay," I had said. "No hard feelings." I hadn't really believed her, though. She liked to say things to try to get me going. Also, I was locked into a strategy of appearing calm and reasonable. You've heard of killing people with kindness. Once Maureen had accused me of killing her with calmness. But I didn't want to get drawn in. If there was only one hothead in the relation-ship, if only one of us threw dishes and stomped out of family Thanksgiving dinner and flirted with other people and slept with other people and threatened to leave for someone else, if only one of us acted crazy like that, I figured the relationship had a fighting chance. I had figured wrong, but even at the very moment she was dumping me and I was starting to see the brutal light, I clung dopishly to my cool cucumber tactic.

Anyway, water under the bridge. That was then. Now

Maureen was marrying Bob and I was fine with that. I did think as we were sitting there and I was looking at the sharp corners of her mouth and her perfectly straight nose, I did think, This is a woman who has said she loves me. I'm sitting with someone who has made silly noises by filling her cheeks with air and exhaling with her mouth against my belly button. I should be angry at her, disappointed maybe, but then, I had said and done a lot of corny romantic things too. Sitting there with her on the morning of her and Bob's wedding, I could barely remember what I said or did or what I meant by it. Six months earlier, I probably would have married her, but for now, I could at least enjoy the fact that she was the one who had let me down, that she was the one who had lied and cheated, not me. Rejection hurts, but I don't like to be the bad guy. I kind of felt sorry for Maureen because she was the one who had to justify herself now. I imagined her with three or four bald, jock kids while I was out living, for lack of a better word, authentically.

At first we talked about safe topics. We reminisced about the red packets of non-dairy creamer they used to have at the Koffee Klutch before the owner had felt the need to go upscale. Now the real cream sat on the table all day, getting warm and sometimes curdling in those lidded metal pitchers better suited for hot water or tea. Maureen was antsy, though, and not in the mood for chit-chat.

"I'm starving," she said, aggressively, as if her hunger were somehow my fault.

"Hrmmfh. Yes," I said helplessly. "Me too," even though I knew agreeing with Maureen never placated her and sometimes drove her to violence.

The silence was intense, aggressive even, until I leaned in as if I were listening earnestly, as if we were having a frank, basically friendly conversation about something safe and external like the new Julia Roberts movie or how ignorant George Bush is. My act was not for Maureen's sake, but for the plump but still attractive woman at the table across from us who was reading the paper and absently scratching a red patch on the side of her neck—eczema, maybe, or an old sunburn. Maureen, you might say, was a lost cause, but all of a sudden it mattered that this woman not find me ridiculous.

"Just take it easy, Maureen," I said, wincing at the jovial, patronizing tone that clutches my voice whenever anyone is angry with me.

Maureen is really quite unattractive when she's angry. She clenches herself tight like a rebellious teenage anorexic at an all-night buffet. Even her lips look too thin and her eyelids flutter at an alarming rate. "Kevin, I really shouldn't tell you this," she began.

I knew she would tell me anyway. The woman with the newspaper was rustling in her purse, getting ready to leave. Maybe, with the right attentive facial expression, I could stall Maureen's outburst until the other woman was gone. I sat back a little, straightened up as if I were comfortable and began nodding my head rapidly as though I was anticipating her words with great excitement. Some dogs thump their tails on the floor when they expect a biscuit. Some men nod their heads when they expect a drubbing.

"I shouldn't tell you this, but I think it's important that you hear it." She paused, but only to fill her lungs with air, not to temper her assault. "I felt bad for a while leaving you for Bob on such short notice and all. I thought maybe it was inconsiderate or selfish, but I see now that you brought it on yourself. Any woman would have done the same thing. I just want to tell you so that there's some hope for you the next time around. I mean, if you ever get another girlfriend. You should know. There's something about you that makes women reject you."

A braver man might have said, *and what might that be?* But I kept silent, although the involuntary nodding ceased as abruptly as it had begun.

"It's—like—your aura or something. It's so thorough, you can practically smell it. Most men project strength or competence or intelligence or something. You just project this, I don't know, this—lack."

"Lack? I project lack?"

"That's exactly it." Maureen sat back, relieved that she had found the precise word. She almost instantly resumed her vivacious, wedding-day appearance.

I might have asked her for more detail. Lack of what? Income? Character? Basketball offense skills? Luckily, our food arrived just then. Grateful for the ritual of eating and that the storm had passed, I checked my urge to greet the waitress as if she were a long-lost relative. Instead, I gave her a measured smile, using the opportunity of glancing up to confirm that Eczema-Neck had mercifully left the diner. The eggs Benedict was better than usual—the eggs just right—neither too hard nor too soft—and the sauce creamy and with just enough zip.

The ceremony was held in a tiny, wooden Lutheran church on Sable Street in Mississauga. Neither Bob nor Maureen was Lutheran, but when they stumbled across the quaint leftover building during a bicycle tour of important Mississauga landmarks, they had pounced on it the same way they scooped up genuine antique knick-knacks from the piles of useless junk at flea markets. The hundred or so guests who were crammed into the hard oak pews to witness Maureen and Bob's nuptials seemed to strain the floorboards of the creaking old vault, almost to its breaking point.

The temperature in the church was about a hundred degrees which made the wedding guests' job of listening attentively and appreciatively all the more challenging. Maureen and Bob had written their own secular vows, church wedding notwithstanding. The vows were thorough, but not really poetic or romantic. Maureen promised to faithfully share home maintenance and other tasks. Bob promised to be *there* for Maureen as a friend, lover, listener and fellow toiler in the drudgery of daily life. Maureen promised not to stand in Bob's way as he made his journey to becoming more fully himself. Both talked about the mutual space they would share and the individual space they would continue to respect and cherish. I imagined both parties were rival diplomats listing their final compromise positions, which had allowed them to narrowly avoid a state of war. It was impossible to tell when, if ever, they might be ready to sum it up with the big "I do."

I sat in the aisle seat of a packed pew, careful not to rub my suit jacket against the glistening arm of the woman next to me. My back was stuck to my dress shirt, which seemed glued to my jacket. From where we were sitting, I could see Bob's face beaming with sweat. Maureen appeared to take the heat well, but Bob was gasping a little and looked more and more in pain. A bright blue vein on his shiny forehead emerged and appeared to throb. It seemed impossible that he would make it to the end, if indeed there was an end to the ceremony. Bob was apparently in the home stretch, extolling his commitment to the loving upkeep of Maureen's cat, BoBo, when the heat finally got the better of him. His knees buckled and he reeled forward in a dead faint onto the minister, who, at last, had a purpose in the ceremony: he caught Bob and eased him to the floor.

The women in the church gasped and leaned forward. A few of the men guffawed abruptly, but most sat bolt upright, blinking and breathing evenly so as to protect themselves from the same fate as Bob. Some Good Samaritans leapt a few pews to administer first aid. Bob came to quickly. A blond little boy in a yellow suit gave him a juice box and Bob was able to drink from the straw. The wedding party helped Bob get back on his feet. Once it was clear that he was still with us, the church became raucous with guests telling their own amusing wedding anecdotes and chuckling over how Bob and Maureen would remember this moment in their golden years. The glowing woman next to me announced to no one in particular or perhaps to me that passing out at your wedding, in her part of the world, is a sign of good luck, though she herself had waited until the reception. The groom's brush with danger had made intimates of all the guests. I gave my pew-mate a warm, appraising glance. She was about thirty-five with a slim, bony figure and black hair mussed just-so. The dress she wore was short and frilly, too young for her, I thought, but she was pretty enough. She wore no wedding ring and her beautiful, graceful hands were marred only by a bright yellow nicotine stain on her index finger. I wondered what sort of good luck her marriage had brought. I said I hoped I might stay conscious for my wedding, but that the woman I married must agree to air conditioning and concise vows.

She looked at me with a hostile smile, her upper lip twitching evocatively.

"I'm Kevin," I said, holding out my hand.

"I'm Gay," she answered, turning her head abruptly to watch the service that was resuming.

The minister deftly steered the delirious couple through the maze of final promises. Bob kissed Maureen and the guests cheered and whooped as if he had just completed a last-quarter touchdown pass. As Bob and Maureen went off to sign the official papers and leave the sauna-like church, Bob's strapping, seventeen-year-old jockette sister stood up in her peach chiffon number, cued the organist and sang in a shaky but still forceful voice, "We've Only Just Begun."

After the stifling heat of the church and tedious precision of Maureen and Bob's vows, the reception was a breeze. We stood around the empty, mildewy, cedar hot tub in Bob's parents' back yard and ate and drank and made small talk. It was still only mid-afternoon, not mealtime, so the appetizers—cheese and crackers, some grapes and an array of Superstore-reheated-from-frozen popovers with the red wine and the keg of beer—felt like enough of a celebration.

I gossiped with old friends of Maureen's and mine and kept a distant eye on Gaylene, the woman of the yellow finger. Gaylene appeared to get quite hammered on a very few glasses of wine and found a seat for herself on Greg Demore's lap. It appeared that Greg, a middle-aged, greying chiropractor colleague of Bob's, was pretending to be Lewis Carroll, while Gaylene played the wide-eyed, innocent Alice. Greg whispered things in her ear that made her blush, and bounced and tickled her while she squirmed and let out intermittent squeaky shrieks.

I observed these shenanigans while I caught up with Lisa Carlyle, a friend from graduate school. It was Lisa, in fact, who had first introduced me to Maureen.

"Well, if it isn't Lisa Carlyle," I said, the way people do at weddings.

"It isn't," she replied, apparently miffed. "Not any more."

"So then, you're married now? Is that the lucky guy?" I asked pointing with my wineglass at a youngish fellow wearing a grim, stiff smile, who was sitting beside us, watching other people eat, talk and dance.

"No, I'm not married. I'm Mary Beth Carlyle now. Nobody calls me Lisa any more."

"Not even your parents?"

"I'm trying to break free of that birth family obligation thing."

"I see. I see," I said, afraid to ask but deadly curious about what sordid family secret caused Lisa to cast her perfectly useful name into the sea and go fish for another one. Perhaps the great aunt she had been named for had come out shamelessly for Intelligent Design over Evolution. Or maybe Lisa/Mary Beth's therapist had helped her remember the unspeakable things her father had done to her while her mother stood by, smoking and buffing her nails. Who knows, but those kinds of stories sometimes make good poems, though usually they are too earnest and appear beside other too-earnest poems in well-funded women's literary journals.

I couldn't look at Lisa/Mary Beth's perky, pleasant face, framed as it was by the same mousy perm she had worn since grad school. I had always liked her—she was a nice, average girl—but I had never found her attractive. While she talked about her job, her dislike for Kate Winslet, her apartment search, I looked past her petite, not so much plump as not quite thin, figure, searching for Gaylene and Greg, or Maureen, or another old friend I had yet to catch up with. Maureen and Bob were dancing salsa in their wedding finery. Every few bars they stopped to link arms and swill champagne. They did an impressive job of playing the happy

23

couple. Gaylene and Greg were dancing too, but though the music was fast, they were dancing slow and were wrapped around each other, so close that Gaylene was actually standing on Greg's feet. They ground together like a couple of kids dancing to "Stairway to Heaven" at a junior high school prom. Maybe it was the wine. Maybe it was the ritual of the wedding or the Latin music blaring from the CD player in Bob's parents' back yard. Maybe it was all those things, but I couldn't take my eyes off Gaylene. Her eyes were closed, her mouth was open and she was gyrating against Greg's paunch like she was about to bring herself off. The rings of frills on her skimpy dress shimmered against her tiny ass, making it look meatier than it probably was.

"So you and I are the single ones, then," I said to Mary Beth, trying to bring the conversation around to something safe.

"Yeah. Don't you hate going to all these weddings? If they're so goddamn happy, what do they need an audience for?"

"The real reason I came to this wedding," I told her, "was to see old friends. Friendship, after all, is more substantial than what passes for romance." I tried to look directly at Lisa/Mary Beth, but found it difficult. She had on a lot of foundation, possibly to cover up scars or a mid-life acne out-break, and the result was that her skin looked soft and pale like old Elmer's glue. Luckily she was short and I could look just over her head and watch the action behind her without appearing to let my attention wander.

"It's so good to see you, Mary Beth," I ventured, not even stumbling over the new name. "We really should keep in touch." The song ended and several guests whooped and cheered for Bob and Maureen. Bob's friends shouted sporty things like, "Way to go, Bobbie," and "Let's go, Maureen an' Bo, Let's go." Greg and Gaylene, oblivious to everything around them, had waltzed over to a picnic bench where Gaylene stumbled on top of Greg. They continued their dance contortions from a horizontal position. Looking past Mary Beth, I could see all the way up Gaylene's stocking to the white diamond centre (cotton, I suppose) that protected what could be called her *love resource centre*. I was so aroused, I was starting to sway on my heels the way half-mad old women with nothing visible left to live for did at my mother's Baptist Revival meetings. Luckily, my dress pants and suit jacket were sufficient for masking my symptom.

The DJ cut the music and all of us settled down to listen to the speeches. Bob's mom went first, choking up when she talked about gaining a daughter. Maureen stared, enraptured, at Bob's mother like she was at a rally listening to Martin Luther King give his "I Have a Dream" speech. Gaylene and Greg managed to sit upright for the speeches, but I could see him working his experienced chiropractor fingers along her rib cage. She squirmed spasmodically, not in discomfort, but in grateful little bursts of affirmation. Spontaneously, I put my arm around Mary Beth and planted my hand on her hip. She moved closer and leaned her head against my shoulder. We stood tight against each other like that while we listened to Bob's brother (best man) and Maureen's sister (maid of honour) sing the happy couple's praises. Then Maureen said she was sad that her dad couldn't be here on this special day, but she wanted to call on an old friend to say a few words. She asked me to come to the microphone.

I felt unhinged. Maureen hadn't mentioned that I was the stand-in for her dad at the wedding.

"Friends," I began and paused to clear my throat and think

of something to say. I spied Gaylene on the picnic bench. She was still entwined with Greg, but except for the cigarette she was dragging on, I had her full attention. Her hair was only slightly messier than it had been at the church and from where I stood, I could see the hard little muscles in her forearms. "Friends and family. There is so much love in this little suburban back yard that I am quite tongue-tied," I said. "I wish Bob and Maureen all the happiness they deserve and then some."

"Way to go, Maureen and Bo," the guests chanted back.

"Yes, indeed. Way to go. Maureen, you have taught me a lot about myself and about life. You and Bob have taught me a thing or two about the nature of love and for that I will always be grateful."

Maureen was smiling at me and blushing. Apparently, my speech was exactly what she'd hoped for and more. As I stepped down, she floated over in her flowing gown and gave me a hug. She whispered in my ear, "Kevin, you're a true friend."

Her breath tickled my ear and I felt completely dizzy with confusion and lust and lack. I clung to her in the embrace she had initiated while the guests cheered and gawked. I held on longer than was appropriate and then longer still. She began to fidget and then squirm and then push against my chest. "Kevin," she hissed in my ear, "get the fuck off of me. You're wrecking my dress."

I held tighter and I whispered, "Gaylene, Gaylene. My dream, my dream. Could this be love so early in the evening?"

Maureen raked her nails across my chest and began to gouge. I must have been drunk because, though she drew blood, I hardly felt any pain. Finally I released her and she shook her head at me and narrowed her eyes to let me know she would pay me back for my trespasses later.

The wedding was winding down. Maureen and Bob made

their quiet exit—they had to get started on their honeymoon, everyone said—which meant the guests had permission to leave. I wanted to say goodbye to Gaylene, but couldn't find her. I felt sure she hadn't left with Greg and that comforted me.

As I walked Mary Beth to her car, I thought about trying to start something with her. I thought about kissing her good-bye. I wondered if she had a perfect little white diamond just like Gaylene's at the centre of her nylons. I thought that if only I wasn't a poet, I might have been attracted to her, per-fect diamond or no, and we might have really clicked.

Mary Beth asked me, "Will you look me up the next time you're in Toronto?"

"Sure. No sweat."

"That would be great. We'll go out somewhere."

"Fantastic."

I took the commuter train back downtown and then the subway over to Bob and Maureen's. I would be house-sitting for them while they were in Portugal. As I rode along, I tried to think cheerfully about things. The wedding had been a success. It wasn't every ex-girlfriend who asked her ex-boyfriend to talk at her wedding or who entrusted her house to him while she was on her honeymoon. And Mary Beth seemed to like me, which made me think it possible that other women might too. The indents on my chest from Maureen's freshly manicured nails were not deep. When I got back to Maureen and Bob's, I might write a poem about the heat the little antique Mississauga church had generated. I might invent, for the sake of beauty, a moth in the rafters of the church—his grey silence but undeni-able presence there high in the sweet, musty softness of the aged rafters, and his imperceptibly trembling wings.

I'm Your Frankenstein

We weren't friends any more, but when we were, David and Emily and their kids used to send us a handmade Christmas card every year. Emily and little Natalie did the cover drawings. Inside, David would inscribe an original poem. Once: "Merry we are / In light of each other." Another year "You. Us. We all." David's tiny poems were always clever, almost ironic, but perfectly salutary.

In the old days, David and Emily and Evan and I used to go out together on Friday nights to movies or concerts or plays. Jillian, David's daughter from his first marriage, would babysit. Saturdays, we didn't see them. Saturdays were for housecleaning, haircuts and Natalie's soccer practice. Most Sunday mornings, we would go for breakfast with David and Emily and all the kids.

Our daughter, Alicia, was great friends with their Natalie,

and Josh had a definite pre-teen crush on Jillian. It started when Josh was four and had to have his tonsils out. Jillian, who was fourteen at the time, came with her parents and Natalie to visit him when he was home from the hospital. She brought him a real live white rabbit in an aluminum cage. The rabbit came complete with a head of lettuce, newspaper for the floor of his cage, a box of all-natural rabbit food. David and Emily gave Josh a copy of *Alice in Wonderland*. David told Josh in a solemn whisper that there was a white rabbit in this book with remarkable skills. Josh ended up loving the book almost as much as he loved Whitey the Rabbit.

We saw David and Emily and their kids all the time but the best part of the week was late on Friday, after the show. We would go for coffee and dissect our entertainment. Some nights we saw something that made us resonate with attentive joy. Some nights we saw something that made us laugh. The best nights, both happened. Most nights we were at least pleasantly distracted.

One time, with David and Emily and their friends, Marina and Chris, we went to see a play, *Mary*, that gave bad art several whole new definitions. After the play, in a noisy corner of Bar Eye, we ate and drank and trashed the play. We ran into some other friends who had seen the play earlier in the week and they joined our rollicking demolition.

The play we saw was a version of *Long Day's Journey into Night*. The catch was that it was written from Mary's point of view, though, as Chris argued, so is the original. The other catch was that the play was performed backwards. Not fully backwards like the Beatles' *White Album*, which, when spun backwards, reveals the name of Kennedy's real assassin plus Ringo's favourite flavour of Häagen Dazs. Just backwards scene by scene. So the play we saw opened with Mary Tyrone saying, "We were very happy, for a time," and just flowed from there. By the end, or the beginning, I guess, the Tyrones really were happy (though, as Marina said, the audience was in a near temper-tantrum state of simmering, raging boredom). Mary was not yet an addict, Edmund was not yet deathly ill and there was hope for Jamie.

Backwards, Evan said, he could stand. What he couldn't bear was the beautiful white plaster masks, or heads on sticks, really, that the actors were forced to carry in front of their faces at all times. Evan was outraged for the actors, fine local ones who couldn't say no to a paying gig. There was one, a promising new talent, Alex Anderson, who played Jamie. After the show, when we encountered most of the cast on the stairwell, Alex told us he had volunteered for Habitat for Humanity that afternoon and had mangled his thumb with a hammer. He showed us his thumb, which looked like a ripe, baby eggplant. Even so, he willingly held the plaster head in front of him for the full ninety minutes, mostly with his left hand because his right thumb was throbbing so much.

To make the actors hold the masks, Evan said, was like making them do the scenes in the dark and under water. The masks obscured facial expression, plus they were heavy, hard to balance and made every movement painful. "Not only under water," I said, "but under the Arctic Sea." The play was performed in a small, Spartan studio in one of those majestic brick buildings in the Exchange District of Winnipeg, the kind that is too trendy or too old for heat. You could see your breath as you squirmed on your grey metal bridge chair. I had worn my mitts and kept my jacket on the entire time. When the lights came up, Emily's ears were Santa Claus red and her lips bright blue.

I said how I hated pretentious, pseudo-seriousness that is mistaken for meaning. My husband said a lot of things, most of them witty, all of them superlatives. He said the play made him fantasize about morphing into Charles Adler and writing for *The Winnipeg Sun*. He would write about art as punishment for the leisure classes. Our other friends joined in, mocking the belaboured symbolism of the play. We laughed so hard that sometimes we could be heard over the raging bass of the music. At one point, Evan's face was so red from laughing and his mouth so distorted that he looked like a character from a Dr. Seuss horror movie. His laughter turned into an uncontrolled half-choking wheeze and I had to get him a glass of water and hold it up to his lips. This type of thing went on for a good forty-five minutes and almost made us glad we'd sat through the show.

Some time later that evening when the calamari rings had been passed around and eaten—all but one, left tragically on the plate as an offering to that Canadian goddess of politeness—refills had been offered and accepted, and we had reached the point in a night out when regret settles in. I thought, six people pay twelve dollars to watch an unwatchable play. They cross and uncross their legs, furtively zip and unzip their parkas and wiggle their toes, trying to look intently interested in what is happening on stage a few feet in front of them. Then they reassure the talented but misused actors in the stairwell as everyone makes their retreat. Next, there is the transferring of six clever, middle class, former English majors (now a high school teacher, a librarian, a graphic artist, two stay-at-home moms/writers and one accountant for CKW, a local television station that plays almost all American sitcoms) from the crowded, noisy theatre to the frozen dark of a Winnipeg downtown Saturday night, to their various Honda Civics, Ford Vibes and one very shameful Chevy Ventura minivan, finding parking for each vehicle (my spot, mine!) and then out into the cold again. All to get to Bar Eye, Corydon's most popular age-, gender- and income-blending watering hole to replay, in hilarious, but minute, detail, the flaws of a play that only ever aspired to be popular with timidly educated, bravely intellectual types like ourselves.

At some point I became dimly aware that David and Emily hadn't really participated in the conversation. They had nodded and smiled and ordered. They'd called David's adult daughter, Jillian, on the cellphone, traded off making agreeable gestures and passed the sugar, but that was all. This wasn't alarming for Emily, who always sat Buddha-like and blissful and even more so when she was well along in a pregnancy, as she was now. She was a great listener, a delightful deferrer who made everyone feel gratefully acknowledged just by her beaming, attentive expression. David was also exceedingly polite, but his politeness had an ironclad quality to it, a tinniness, really. His silence echoed through the room. Finally the rest of us shut up all at once. Probably we were just catching our breath or maybe we were having a collective black hole moment. We prided ourselves on never running out of things to say. For whatever reason—exhaustion, emptiness, timing—there was a pause and David used it to clear his throat. "I thought the play was superb," he said.

He explained patiently to us the subtleties of the play: the brilliance of the acting ("Yes, yes," we demurred, "they are all fine actors"); the way the blind plaster heads on sticks represented the characters' blindness to each other; the way the time reversal forced the audience to actually hear the tragic beauty in every line.

We said how amazing the lines were.

"I love that, 'I invented you. You're my Frankenstein,'"

Emily put in delicately, supporting David, but not necessarily disagreeing with us, either.

We half listened as David went on, going over in our minds the venomous things we had said about the play that could now not be taken back. We listened to David patiently explain to us why Mary was worth reverence, not ridicule, and though we nodded and *mmm hmmmed* gently, we felt ashamed. We felt like frat boys whose secret life has been exposed to the world and critiqued by one of their own.

I was thankful that it was dark in Bar Eye and the music was getting louder. For a while, I tuned David out altogether and tried to make out the lyrics to the Weakerthans song grinding away. Something about one of those days when you *wanna* try heroin. Something about scars and bikes and the Tao of questions. I watched Emily and suspected that she, like me, was zoning out and letting the boys duke it out; flying high on the anger and chaos and pounding rhythm of the music.

Though we had been best everything at their wedding (man and woman) and were called first after the grandparents when Josh and Natalie were born, by the time Emily had Brock, we were so out of touch, we only learned about the baby from Chris and Marina. I had weathered difficulties in other friendships before and even chosen to let some friends go. But Emily was so sweet and David so bright with his shiny forehead and earnest, polite, intense need to understand and articulate everything. They were our main "couple friends" and without them, we suddenly felt as raw and alone as if we were back in junior high. For months we tried to get together with them, but every Sunday morning, they had a reason not to go for breakfast and every Friday night they were frantically busy, "doing work around the house," as David put it, though their house was immaculate and David was useless at home repairs anyway.

At the end of most days, when our kids were finally asleep, the house returned to its neutral state of minimal order, and Evan and I were in bed reading or vying for the latest issue of *The New Yorker*, all conversation came around to David and Emily. It was so bad that the first thing we said after making love (well, the second thing after "I love you, Honey" or "That was great") was, "Why do they hate us? What did we do?"

"I think it's me," Evan would say. "It's not you, Honey. It's just some macho thing because he doesn't make as much money as me."

Secretly, I thought it was him. It was that face Evan made when he laughed or the way he always sat there dumbly when the cheque came as though nothing was required of him, until I kicked him under the table and he would say in a mournful, barely audible voice, "Let me get that. I think it's my turn."

But I would say, "No, Honey. It isn't you. Maybe it's the kids. It's been years since Alicia bit Natalie but Emily told me once, she still has a scar. They think I let the kids run wild. Or maybe it's me—she must hate that I'm skinny while she's bloated and ruining her legs with another pregnancy."

"It's not you, Sweetie," he would say, but I could see him thinking, *plausible. Quite plausible.*

We couldn't get off the subject. David and Emily avoided us fastidiously and we imagined more and more outlandish reasons why. We imagined postpartum depression for Emily, a secret tumour for David, marital trouble, a gambling addiction, a job demotion.

"Shouldn't we, you know, confront them? Beg for their forgiveness or something?"

"Guys don't do that kind of thing. But send them something for the baby. We don't want to offend them."

"Why the hell don't we want to offend them? I'm upset. I want them to be upset."

"Don't wind yourself up, Honey. You'll just make yourself sick over it."

It was as though that evening at the movie and Bar Eye had been designed by David as a moral fable. We were the too-sly foxes or the too-greedy grubs who had taken the bait from the clever cow. Like the animals in those stories, we were too base to be expected to even learn anything from our mistakes. We were the bad examples. The most acknowledgement we could hope for was punishment in the form of shunning.

One night we invited Chris and Marina over, ostensibly for dinner, but really so we could grill them about David and Emily. Marina told us she had stopped in for a minute after work to see Emily and drop off a baby gift. She said Emily was looking like her old self (translation: barely fat at all after just giving birth). She said the baby was a power sleeper and Natalie hadn't yet suggested that they "send it back" or tried murdering it in its sleep. "All good signs," Marina said.

Chris said he'd had lunch with David a few times. Apparently, David had loved *Mystic River*. The last time we'd called to invite them to a Friday night movie, they hadn't returned our call and we had gone to that. "We loved it too," I said, my lip quivering. For some reason their loving the film replaced my sense of shame and betrayal with surging fury.

Marina put her arm around me, enjoying her status as the better friend by default. Now that I'd shown my weakness, it was her turn to go in for the kill under the guise of giving compassionate advice. "Just talk to them," she crooned. "They love you guys. You know how it is with a new baby."

I wriggled out from under Marina's arm and went to get the coffee. "We'll see," I said.

Once, about a year after the Bar Eye fiasco, we ran into them in the Salisbury House restaurant parking lot. I cooed over the baby but didn't look either Emily or David in the eye. Josh, now eight and in a hostile-to-the-world phase, looked at them coolly, but refused to say hello. Natalie and Alicia raced at each other and whooped and hugged like Natalie was Oprah and Alicia was Gayle King. David and Emily took the girls' lead. They beamed at us and said things like "It's been so long" and "We've sure missed you guys."

Evan said, "Why is that? If you're so glad to see us, why did you dump us?"

David looked tense and compassionate and hurt and Emily looked like she always does—serene, like she is a cloud about to pull apart into tiny white wisps.

"We've been busy," David said. "I've been working."

"What work?" Evan said. David had a nine-to-five job he left at the office.

"My work," David repeated, his smile freezing into a grimace.

"But it is so wonderful to see you," Emily said.

I took Alicia's hand and clutched it so hard that she hovered a few inches above the ground. With her in tow, I turned around and marched away from them. "I'll see you inside, Evan," I managed to grind out over Alicia's screams.

Evan stood outside in the wind-whipped lot, talking with them for a long time. When he finally came in, he looked weary. "They seem completely unaware that there has even been a rift."

"I'm done with them," I said. "Done."

"I wanna sit with Natalie," Alicia said and she bounded across the restaurant to the booth where Natalie, the baby and her parents were settling in. After a few minutes, I sent Evan to retrieve her. She came willingly, thank God.

We didn't see them after that, but I did drop off a baby gift. It was a sweater that Emily's mother had made for Alicia when she was born. It was yellow and had little yellow duck buttons on it. It would just fit the new baby. I put it in the box that had held Whitey, Josh's rabbit, in the freezer since Alicia had fed it a box of Advil and it died in its sleep. She didn't do it on purpose; she's only a little girl and she didn't know she was hurting Whitey. Anyway, he died peacefully, we'd told Josh. I didn't bother to remove Whitey from the box when I tucked the baby sweater in it, but Whitey was frozen and didn't stink. I wrapped up the box in wrapping paper with little pink and blue teddy bears on it. I thought about writing a card, but I really had nothing to say, so I didn't.

At Christmas when we still didn't hear from them, Evan finally figured out what we'd done. "It was the cards," he said. "The little one-liners David wrote. I think he considers himself a poet. I should have said more about them. I should have praised his little poems." All that stuff about how brilliant the play was and our inability to recognize it was really about our not recognizing David.

"Maybe," I said to Evan. "So what's her excuse? Who needs friends like that, anyway?"

Trespassers

Georgia was not Andrew's first love. Years ago, he had loved Jenny in spite of her inverted nipple and her cloudy red eye. He had offered to give up everything for her, and she had laughed and said, "Give up what? Your UI check? Your roach-infested apartment? Your so-called personality? Your principles? Don't do it on my account, Honey."

But he would have done anything on her account. He invested all of himself in her account. His heart, body and soul were sunk in the bank of Jenny. When she left him, he proved his devotion by smashing all the glasses and empty liquor bottles in his apartment (which was a lot of glass, enough to cover the entire living room), and then lying down and rolling himself across it. Weeks after, little bits of glass still festered near the surface of his skin and then erupted like leftover party favours. His love for Jenny was a test of his character—he tried to continue loving her forever, even after years had passed and the slivers of glass had dislodged and become lost and the scabs had turned to scars and faded into nothing. He believed that his feelings mattered, if not to Jenny, then at least in some larger way. His feelings would make him someone special, someone real, someone who was like indelible ink on someone else's heart. But they didn't, and after awhile even Andrew grew bored with his feelings for Jenny. They had become more like reminiscences of feelings than living, bruising, bleeding feelings. Jenny had long since forgotten Andrew and moved in with the lead singer for Oh, Mama, Mama, a local heavy metal group, and she had a kid they'd named something unforgivable, like Hunter or Drum.

Andrew started acting with a small theatre company and liked the thrill of becoming someone else on stage. It didn't pay very well, and he supported himself by working as a bouncer for raves and selling ecstasy and uppers to the kids. He prided himself on never sampling his own wares and almost never screwing the cute little lollipop faces who would do anything for another hit.

When Georgia joined the theatre company, Andrew was not in the mood for love. He saw right through Georgia's pretty young wife/struggling actress routine. She was selfish, empty and not to be trusted. Gradually, these qualities grew on him and he started to recognize that, like himself, she was a sealed vessel of pain floating through life in need of a rock upon which to smash herself open. She was dreaming her life, not living it, and he wanted to help her live it.

One night, the theatre troupe did a cabaret as a fundraiser for their upcoming touring show of *Dogs*, the mock sequel to *Cats*. Andrew and Georgia did a Simon and Garfunkel take-off together. Georgia wore a curly yellow wig and Andrew strummed a guitar, and they belted out the chorus to, "I Am a Rock." As Andrew hit the final chords, they looked into each other's eyes in that knowing, mushy way folk singers always do at the end of a number and they fell madly in love. Georgia's husband, Victor, a financial planner and lover of opera and forties movies, sat in the audience stone still, glassy-eyed and with a smile of pride rigid on his face. The rest of the audience roared with laughter, boos and catcalls. Victor's smile was so blissfully repressive, so chock-full of denial, that it seemed clear to Andrew that Victor was aware that Andrew was the better man for Georgia. Once he'd had time to think it through, Victor would see that Andrew and Georgia belonged together.

After the show when Victor went straight home (the babysitter had a geometry test the next morning and couldn't stay late), Andrew helped Georgia drink enough bourbon straight up that it wouldn't be her fault whatever happened. What happened was they walked home, arm in arm, staggering and singing and clinking invisible glasses. By the time they were passing the park on the corner of her street, Georgia's head was starting to clear. She puked in the bushes and then she and Andrew crawled under a tree and groped each other for what seemed like hours. They were covered in evidence— grass stains, dirt, leaves and litter, but felt pretty decent about not actually *doing it*. Andrew went home and slept for thirty-six hours straight.

Georgia went home and looked at her children, Robin and Adam, sleeping like little cherubs. Then she went in to her own bedroom, woke Victor up and told him that she loved the children and she loved Victor, but she had fallen in love with Andrew and her marriage to Victor was over. "You've had too much to drink," he told her, and he started undressing her and pushing her not too gently onto the bed. He made love to her without asking if it felt all right for her or if she came or if she loved him. It did feel all right for her, because she was thinking about Andrew and how he would know how to make her really, truly, finally and fully herself. Victor told her he loved her and that they would work things out, that she was probably premenstrual and tired too. She hugged him and told him she would miss him a lot and really miss the kids. He pushed her off him and went down to the living room to watch something black and white and full of shadows and revenge on the Turner Movie Classics station.

Georgia had to decide what to wear to the counselling session. It was too cold out for her dignified but hip-hugging sunny yellow skirt. It would be wrong for her to wear jeans or anything too disrespectful. Even her shirt with the one word, *esprit* emblazoned across the chest, though meant to suggest an appealing gustiness, would only translate to "Home-Wrecking Slut Feigns Innocence" in the current context.

Georgia was a mother, but so often people still treated her like a child. She was clever, but not the kind of clever that wins you an award or a scholarship. By profession, she was an actress. She was a good actress, sometimes even great, but that just added to the tumbleweed that seemed to be knocking around inside her. Lately, she had played a series of bitchy, unhappy, comic career women. Off stage, she found herself catty and brittle and laughing too loud. Other women found her easy to hate. The feeling was often mutual. What Georgia showed the world about herself was like a collection of hard bits of coloured plastic in a child's kaleidoscope—shake shake shake, and it's a beautiful new flower.

The counselling session had been arranged and paid for by Georgia's recently ex-husband's second stepmother. Patricia, the counsellor, had seen Georgia and Victor separately and had even had a session with Andrew, Georgia's lover and the alleged cause of the breakup. The counsellor now wanted to see Georgia and Victor together. Whenever the counsellor wanted compliance, she began with, "When there are children involved . . ." At Georgia's last session, Patricia had said, "I think I should meet with the two adults together and try to work something out. When there are children involved, crisis needs resolution." Georgia had barked out a laugh. For some reason, the word *resolution* sounded like a particularly piquant kind of Mexican food—*enchilada, quesadilla, resolution.* But she understood that when a mother of two young children takes a lover and abandons her family, she is the one who is required to explain and justify.

Georgia paced around her new, gloriously empty apartment. There were no toys, no furniture, none of the milk, cereal and diaper-bucket smells that had enveloped her these last five years. The floors were shiny hardwood. The walls were white. There were only a few windows, but they were good-sized and gaped nakedly at the street. The emptiness of the rooms made them seem larger and made Georgia feel smaller. "I like it here," she said out loud. "Here I am, at home at my new place," she ventured, and it didn't sound false. She would bring Robin and Adam here to visit soon. When the kids came, the apartment would be like one big oversized playhouse. But for now it was all Georgia's.

The one room in the apartment that was properly furnished was the bedroom. She had a double bed, her grandmother's inlaid oak dresser, which had birds carved around the mirror, a night table, her clothes in the closet, and a few books on the window ledge. She had taken a sheer piece of fabric and tacked it up so that it billowed across the ceiling and along the side of the bed like a tent or a large veil. Lying in bed was like being on the inside of a very good dream. Today, Georgia stopped herself from climbing inside the dream bed because she thought she would never get out. She closed her eyes and felt her way to the closet. With her eyes still rammed shut, she groped for the clothes in the closet and put on the first thing she grabbed—the esprit shirt under an oversized wool sweater which hung almost to her knees and a pair of barely-frayed black leggings.

Victor lay on the couch with the basketball game on low. He had always vaguely disliked sports, but once it seemed clear that Georgia was really gone, he had lost his taste for old movies with their tragic plots, or, worse, impossible happy endings. Now he kept the television permanently on the sports channel as a kind of steady flow of Novocain. Adam, who was two, was trying to teach himself to fly by climbing on to the coffee table and then leaping off. Every time he landed, he squealed and the house shook and the television jumped out of focus. Robin, who was five, sat at Victor's feet, compulsively drawing wedding pictures. The one of Robin and Adam together at the altar, both with their blankees as veils, was so cute that Victor wanted to have it framed.

Victor watched the players running and dribbling and jostling each other up and down the court. They seemed so purposeful. So sure. So fucking tall. If he wasn't careful he would start to hate them all. These days, he had so much hate in him that it was as if his whole body had been tarred with sticky, gooey, invisible hate. Everything he touched or looked at or thought about got mired in it, and he had to drag himself from room to room, along with his hate and the things that were stuck to it pulling him down low to the ground. He felt dirty and heavy, like an animal in a stall. Victor sat up and rolled his head on his shoulders, the way you do to warm up before exercising, except he moved so violently that it looked to Adam like he was trying to fling his head off his shoulders and smash it against the wall.

"Daddy okay? Daddy need hug? Daddy okay?" Adam stood on the coffee table with his arms spread wide, and as he talked he flung himself onto Victor. It isn't a two-year-old's job to comfort his screwed-up parents, but Adam was good at it and it didn't seem to take anything out of him. Victor hugged Adam hard and told him, "Daddy okay."

He was okay. He had to be. Today was the counselling session with Georgia. Today the counsellor would patiently and, in a non-judgmental way, explain to Georgia that she had made a mistake. She could not stop loving Victor. She could not leave them. Things really still were the way they were before. Georgia, with the help of an objective third party, would understand. He would forgive her, because the part of him that wasn't imagining unspeakable horrors for her already had. The part of him that wasn't envisioning Georgia—flabby, old and crying steadily and rattling her wares for the old men who drove around the strip with twenty dollars in their pockets and lust in their hearts—knew that Georgia was really just a kid. If she knew her own mind, it would tell her how much she loved Victor. He would forgive her and her gratitude would see them through. She could stay young and beautiful and even innocent but only as Victor's wife. Without him, blue eye shadow and heavy mascara would start to crop up on her face and she would sprout varicose veins on her twenty-eight-year-old perfect calves. He was her hope. He was her life raft. He was her future. She had to love him or all would be lost.

"Robin, do you want to help Daddy make Mackie Cheesies? Come on. It's almost lunchtime." They went into the kitchen and he helped her fill up the pot with water. Adam came along too, because he would do anything, sometimes even pee in his potty, for Mackie Cheesies. He loved it with salt, pepper and Worcestershire sauce. He was passionate about it. Being in the same room with the smell of just-mixed Kraft Dinner gave him a sense of rapture.

While the kids were eating, Victor's stepmother, Caroline, came over to babysit Adam and Robin so Victor could go to the counselling session. Adam and Robin were fond of her, even though they liked to repeat their nickname for her, "Other-Gram-Other, Other-Gram-Other," over and over until it could only sound like a reproach. They wouldn't stop, even when she begged them to and threatened them with real grandmotherly tears.

"I can out-cry any grandma on the block," she would say and they would yell out, "Cry, Other-Gram-Other, Cry!"

Everything in Patricia's office was carefully chosen and placed to be as friendly and neutral as possible. Three plush, beige armchairs faced off against each other in the centre of the room. The chairs were identical to and equidistant from one another. Grey floor-length vertical blinds concealed a large picture window. Georgia and Victor both stood fidgeting and waiting for Patricia to indicate which chair was hers and which ones were meant for them.

"Please sit down," Patricia said, flashing her disarming smile.

Georgia and Victor stood frozen for a few seconds and then simultaneously darted for the same chair. Victor fairly shoved Georgia out of the way and sat down first.

"This is so much fun," Georgia giggled and sat down in the chair nearest the window.

Patricia sat down too, trying not to reveal her annoyance that Georgia was in her chair. "Shall we get started?" she asked, her hazel eyes flashing back and forth at Victor and then at Georgia.

Patricia found Victor the more likable of the two. He wasn't handsome, but he looked like a good man. He had wrinkles around his eyes from smiling through too much pain. Georgia was beautiful, but nearly drowning in her sweater-dress. She looked like a little girl playing dress-up, Patricia thought. She's not a child, for God's sake. This isn't a game of Twister.

"Who would like to begin?" Patricia asked.

Victor was ready to pounce. "Maybe Georgia could explain to you why she's trying to wreck her life, my life, and destroy our kids."

Patricia leaned in, "Good, Victor. Go ahead, Georgia. Tell us why you're here."

"I guess if I knew that, I wouldn't be here," Georgia said and instantly started sobbing. "I'm trying. I'm really trying," she blubbered.

"Georgia, this isn't about blame. It's about what's best for everyone," Patricia said. Her voice was kind, but there was a deep meanness in what she said. How could there be something that is best for everyone? That was just a crazy, feel-good idea.

Patricia and Victor looked at Georgia and waited patiently for her to say something reasonable. In Patricia's experience, if you waited quietly long enough, most clients would put away the dramatics and focus on the problem. Usually they started with something tiresome like, "What are you, my mother?" but then went on to get down to business. Georgia sat quivering in Patricia's chair for several minutes, staring both Victor and Patricia down. Patricia found it hard to look at Georgia without wanting something from her. Georgia was so fragile and her skin practically translucent. Her hair was shoulder length with blonde highlights where the track lighting caught it. She had a few shorter wisps of hair on her forehead, which wanted to be ringlets. Her eyes were all big brown innocence. She didn't look like a person capable of ever doing harm.

Finally, Georgia stopped trembling and wiping her eyes enough to speak. "I'm here because I want you to love me," she said, looking imploringly not at Victor, but at Patricia. "I know I'm not lovable. I know that. But it just struck me that if you could love me, even though all you know about me is the bad stuff I've done, if you could love me, well, maybe then I might be okay."

Patricia wasn't a sucker. She knew what Georgia was doing. It was client manipulation one-o-one. She was trying to draw Patricia in emotionally—trying to bring her down to where Georgia was. Patricia knew it was her job to remain objective, but when Georgia had said the word *love*, it was suddenly like a summons. Patricia wanted to press her thumbs against Georgia's closed eyes and kiss her forehead. She wanted to touch Georgia's lips. But therapists were supposed to be fair. They weren't supposed to have needs. Patricia's secret albatross was that no matter how hard she struggled against it—and with every calm breath she struggled hard against it—she found marriage counselling massively erotic. Sometimes it was the husband. Sometimes it was the wife. There were times where she had mentally undressed both within minutes of a session. The more the accusations flew, the more seriously they took their pain, the more their voices quavered, the more they jockeyed for her approval, the more aroused she felt. Most clients were too self-absorbed to even notice, but Georgia had taken one look and seen right into Patricia's dirty heart.

"I really think you could help me," Georgia was saying.

Patricia shivered and involuntarily drew back in her chair.

Victor stood up and shouted, "This is total fucking bullshit. Quit acting, Georgia. This isn't a fucking audition."

Georgia pressed her advantage, continuing to ignore Victor and only address Patricia. "He's never been supportive of my career, not really. You understand how hard it is to put yourself out there on stage? To try, to fail, to keep trying with the clock always working against you?"

Patricia didn't really hear what Georgia said but maintained her strategy, which was to carry on with her *we can work it out* script and hope for the best. "What I'm hearing is that both of you want to do whatever it takes to make your family whole again. Is that what I'm hearing?" she asked.

"That's what you're hearing," Victor said and paused, waiting for Patricia to give him points for his calm, reasonable stance. A minute ago he had been screaming at her, but now all his rage was hidden away like the pointed tip of his striped tie, which was tucked neatly into his pleated blue dress pants.

"What I'm hearing," Georgia said. "What *I'm* hearing—" her words were cut off by the sound of a strange voice from behind the blinds echoing her.

"What I'm hearing," the voice echoed. "What I'm hearing."

Victor, Georgia and Patricia were struck dumb as Andrew

emerged from his hiding place between the blinds and the picture window. He was wearing only olive green track shorts, a well-worn Save the Jets t-shirt, sport socks, black patent business shoes and a manic expression on his glowing face. Patricia screamed; she stood up, regained her composure and said, "You'd better leave or I'm calling 911."

"Let us not to the marriage of true minds admit impediments," Andrew said, producing a bouquet of flowers from behind the curtain with the flourish of a magician producing a rabbit. Andrew held out the flowers, dusty plastic peonies, a prop left over from a show, for Georgia's approval.

Patricia said into the phone, "Yes. There's an intruder in my office. Yes. I don't think so, but how would I know? Yes. Thank you. Two-seventeen Balmoral. Suite twelve. It's on the second floor. Yes. Thank you." She put down the phone and told Andrew the police were on their way.

"I'm not dangerous," Andrew said, "just in love. Georgia and I are in love. Is there a law against that?"

Georgia said, "Take it easy, Victor. Take it easy, everyone."

Victor felt justifiably murderous. For the first time in his life there was a living person fully deserving of all his anger standing right in front of him. His whole body rocketed with self-righteous rage as he advanced on Andrew. "You're heinous," he shouted, "You're heinous," except he mispronounced *heinous* so it sounded like he was shouting, "Your Highness, Your Highness." Each time he shouted it, he went for Andrew, pushing him steadily backwards.

Andrew was an actor, not a fighter. He made only a feeble attempt to hold his ground. He pleaded in a small voice that became smaller each time Victor pushed him, "It's love. We're in love. That's nobody's fault, Victor." He backed up every time Victor shoved him. With one final "Your Highness,"

Andrew stepped backwards against the window and the force of his body against the glass shattered it. Andrew was still pleading as he slid through the empty pane and disappeared from view as unexpectedly as he had appeared. In movies when people leaped or were pushed through picture windows, the bystanders gasped and screamed and swooned or rushed to the rescue. No one did any of that. Instead, Patricia guffawed too loudly, while Victor and Georgia did nothing but stare. The sound Patricia made was like someone sneezing vigorously at a funeral. It was the kind of inappropriate sound people remember you for, long after they forget everything else about you. It was Victor who had pushed Andrew out the window, Victor who couldn't control his feelings, but Patricia felt her unruly laugh had implicated her; that Victor and Georgia and even Andrew possibly would see everything as her fault.

Andrew did a little sommersault when he hit the snow and got up moving. He might have turned around for one final soliloquy but the fall or the coldness of the snow had knocked all the romance out of him. Instead he jogged towards the Great West Life parking lot without looking back. By the time Patricia, Georgia and Victor had recovered enough from the shock of Andrew's departure to rush to the shattered window, Andrew was already making his escape. They saw him fighting his way through the snow in remarkable haste, treating parking lot barriers as easy hurdles.

Victor put his arm around Georgia. "Come on, Honey. Let's go home. The kids . . ."

"Thank you for everything, and I'm really, really sorry about this," Georgia told Patricia. Georgia didn't resist Victor shepherding her towards the door.

"Just go," Patricia told them.

Georgia and Victor left the office and Patricia sat down in the chair near where the window had been, the chair where, minutes earlier, Georgia had sat and begun to open up her heart to Patricia. The cold air from outside had already filled up the room and Patricia put her icy hands on her own cheeks and waited for her next appointment.

As Andrew jogged through the Great West Life parking lot, his skin and clothes and hair wet from the snow and his breathing heavy from his fall, he did not feel the cold and he did not believe that things had gone so badly. His love for Georgia was not an act, but like everything in life, it was a performance. As performances go, this may have been his finest hour. Acting was about honesty. The veracity of his performance would almost certainly bring about a major change in Georgia's and Victor's lives (perhaps back to loving each other, perhaps to really going their separate ways, perhaps to something else new and startling and unforeseen but no less genuine). His declaration of love had not caused the walls around everyone to crumble, but they had caused the glass to shatter and allowed Andrew to vanish into the whiteness of Winnipeg winter. As exits go, this too had certainly been his finest. Tumbling out the window and then the shock of the packed snow was the only way to end a show. From now on, all his performances would end this way. As he manoeuvred through the parked cars and edged himself over the short wooden fences designed to discourage trespassers like himself, he realized that the elation he was feeling had little to do with Georgia. He did love her, but somehow his good fortune at being allowed to properly tell her so freed him of the humdrum, repetitive parts of being in love. It was good to love her but just as good to love her while he was wet, freezing, underdressed and alone. In pure love, there was no need for sex, laundry, arguments and bank loans.

As Andrew jogged past the Granite Curling Club, he saw Victor and Georgia driving up to the stop sign in Victor's Saab. They had to drive right past him and then to sit at the stop sign and wait for a chance to merge into the traffic moving on the Osborne Street Bridge. It was late in the afternoon and the cars were bumper-to-bumper going over the bridge. No matter how much Andrew slowed down his pace, it was impossible not to overtake them. Rush hour at the corner of Mostyn and Osborne was one of those rare situations where pedestrians have the edge over cars. If he stood still, he would freeze to death. When he approached their car, he saw Georgia was looking at Victor, perhaps in animated conversation. As he passed the car, he saw Victor slam his hands down on the steering wheel, as in fury or delight at something Georgia had said. It was delicious not to know what was being said but only that it was a part of their ongoing and newly rekindled conversation. He couldn't tell if they were laughing or fighting. Andrew gave a little wave, the kind you give to someone you think you know but aren't quite sure. It was a kind of insurance wave, in case some gesture was expected of him but easy to ignore or dismiss if nothing so dramatic was required. Andrew jogged ahead of the car and around the bend onto the bridge, elated not to know whether Georgia and Victor had seen his gesture or responded to it.

After the Credits

The phone rings at eight in the morning while I have Chris in the bath. I can't leave him there alone. "Come on, Chris, hurry up. Daddy's on the phone." I pull him out and try to dry him with the towel on the floor, which is still wet from my shower. He struggles, almost slipping out of my hands as I run down the hall to the kitchen. "You're a pain, Chris," I tell him. I pick up the telephone and say hello to a dial tone.

On her day off, Ann comes over with Lise and Liam around nine and we have coffee. Lise and Liam are supposed to be company for Chris but they don't get along. Chris hugs one of his cars and tries to stay out of the way. Lise or Liam rips the car out of his hand and chucks it. Chris decides not to cry. Liam and Lise forget about him and fight over a Fisher-Price learning toy—a whole little town. Liam won't give Lise the mailman. Lise knocks over everything in the fire hall.

Ann's policy is to let Liam and Lise work out their problems themselves. I don't blame her. Just Chris alone when he's sulky is usually more than I can handle.

I met Ann at Ace when I worked there and I also met Steve and Doug there. Steve is Chris's father. We are all commercial artists, which is another thing. Steve and Doug have been friends forever.

Ann and I used to talk about her husband, Doug, all the time. Before he was her husband. We'd have coffee at a different time from everyone else, just by accident, so we could talk about him. The first thing Ann would say is, "What can you say about Doug? I should appreciate him."

Ann credits me with helping her get serious about Doug. She would say, "How can I know the future?" and I'd say, "Get serious, Ann. What are you waiting for?"

We never talked about Steve then. He was kind of my secret. Some Fridays after work, payday I guess, Steve and I would go to a bar. Steve, who never said a word to me all day at work, sure could talk. He had plans. He wasn't really a commercial artist. Words like *commercial* and *artist* were shit. He was just filling up time. All you had to do, he said, was hand out the dynamite and he'd light out of town. Some big city where nobody knows anything about anybody else and he could splash himself in red and blue and green across every building and billboard on every street. While he talked this way, we would both get pretty drunk and then he'd drive me home and we'd make out on my carpet. Whenever he kissed me, he had this kind of ritual where he would hold the back of my head with both hands and slide his cheek across mine. He had these Harlequin Romance sandpaper cheeks. On Mondays he would brush past me like Friday hadn't existed. We were co-conspirators.

56

I didn't want to let Ann in on it, but once, after she and Doug were already living together, she said without any prompting, "Steve will come around."

He did, but it took a few years. Not until after I got pregnant with Chris. We bought this house and everything was fine except Steve never could figure out how I got pregnant. I mean, he thought it was something I did to him. But he told me all those plans were shit and that arrogance was shit and that he could get up in the morning and go to work every day as well as Doug could. He'd been doing it for about as long, hadn't he?

For me, it was like after the ending to a Hollywood movie. We had this house and there was Chris kicking around inside me, ballooning bigger and bigger, and Steve coming home from work, kissing me systematically: forehead, mouth, belly-button. I'm not much of a doubter, but after the credits is no time to doubt. I didn't miss going to work at all. I was bloated with anticipation.

Now Ann and I talk about the kids, and what Chris and I are going to do. I am glad she is here for the distraction, if nothing else. I wish we could go on about Doug the way we did at Ace. Her wanting to help makes me nervous. It's like I was a bystander to some event and then they turned the television cameras on me. I should have something clever to say. It's expected.

"You can work. Chris is old enough for daycare," she says.

"I've done some freelancing, " I say. "Not much. With the baby ..."

Chris knows when someone's talking about him. He comes over and climbs on my lap and tries to pull up my shirt to nurse. He is eighteen months old and hasn't nursed since his first birthday, but he still tries sometimes. I hold him and give him a cracker. Liam and Lise are playing house in the doghouse. Steve and I were going to get a dog, a golden retriever, as soon as Chris was old enough. Liam and Lise are shouting at each other, but it's only a play fight. Ann and I have to raise our voices to hear each other.

The phone rings. "Jeez," I say to cover for the panic in my throat. "I wonder what they're selling." It's a man's voice; no one I know.

"Ann?" he says.

"Just a minute," I say.

"Hi," Ann says.

"I'm not playing in your stupid doghouse," Lise shouts.

"Lise, honey, keep it down, Mummy can't hear," Ann says, covering the receiver of the phone. To the phone she says, "Yeah, I know," nodding her head. "I know, I know," each word a little higher pitched than the last. "I want to see you too." For some reason her tone sets me on edge, and I'm thinking, why did I invite this woman and her two monster children into my house? Did I really think she might have something to say to me?

"I can't," Ann says. "Nursery school is tomorrow from nine until lunchtime. We can talk then. I'll see you. Okay."

Ann hangs up the phone, looks at me and looks down. I realize I am staring at her as if she has just committed some unforgivable sin and we are both embarrassed. Just for something to do, I smile and Ann sits up straighter, as if she has just noticed a stranger in the corner, a man, watching her.

"You can manage without Steve," she says, as if she's suddenly remembered I'm the one we're supposed to talk about today.

I slide Chris off my lap and try to change the subject. I don't want to know about the mystery caller. I couldn't care less. "How's Doug, anyway?" I ask.

"You know, nice. Really nice. I can't stand him. No, not

really. The kids are madly in love with him. They say, Mom, you're such a grouch. Why can't you play with us like Daddy does? Yesterday I actually told Lise that it bores the hell out of me to play Snakes and Ladders with her. She couldn't figure that one out."

She's challenging me, like she expects me to say, that's great, Ann. I admire your honesty or something.

I pour us more coffee, which takes the pressure off. We hold our warm mugs and sip. Lise, or maybe it's Liam, is crying, but Ann is oblivious.

"He'll call," I say.

"What?" Ann says.

"Steve. He'll call. He's just got to figure some things out."

"Sure," she says.

Lise has stopped crying. She has pulled off one of the runners that hangs from my spider plant by the television. She is going for the other one, so Ann jumps up and grabs her. "Here's a flower, Mum," she says, holding up the plant.

"No, it's a spider plant, Lise."

"Flower," she says, smelling it.

Ann swings her around and tries to get her interested in something else. "Come show Chris your flower."

"Chris piss," she says. Liam laughs and says, "Chris priss." They keep laughing and saying it. Even Chris is laughing. "Chris piss Chris priss Chris piss."

"Shut up," I shout. "Shut up. You've got no right." Everyone is quiet, staring at me. It is as if the house is frozen with fear and we are all trembling.

"He's been gone a week now, Deb," Ann says, but I don't want to hear her.

"I bet you kids want some lunch," I say. "Come on in the kitchen."

For lunch they have cottage cheese, raisins and Alphagetti. Chris buries his hand in the noodles and sucks them off his fingers. Liam opens his mouth and orders Lise to throw raisins in it. "Don't you dare," Ann says.

"Just eat," I say, "just eat."

Ann helps me scrape the dishes and put them in the sink. She has to take Liam to the eye doctor.

I'm glad when they finally leave. Chris cries, wanting them to stay.

The telephone rings. I stare at it. Chris is sleeping on the carpet in front of the television. Game shows always put him to sleep. I guess he likes the background noise. When he wakes up he will have the imprint of the pattern of the carpet on his face.

The phone rings again and I go to answer it.

"Hello."

"Hi. My name is Melanie. Are you the lady of the house?"

I can't believe this nothing call. "No," I shout. "No, I'm not."

"Oh, um, sorry, um . . ." She is so flustered she hangs up on me before I have a chance to do it first. She sounded so young; probably her first real job. I should feel sorry for her. She isn't going to last long.

I change Chris while he's lying there, hoping it will wake him up. He stirs to make it easier for me to get the old diaper off, but stays asleep. I get up and look at the little town. I put the mailman inside the post office, the fire truck in the fire hall. I put the nozzles in their slots on the gas pumps. I fold the two halves of the town together and close the latch. I pick up Chris's cars and put them in a line on top of the radiator. I think I hear a car slowing down outside. I keep listening until I hear it pull up next door and the engine clicks off.

I walk into the kitchen and stare at the dishes in the sink: a week's worth. I just rinse what I need. From the kitchen I hear Chris waking up. "Kiss piss," he says, because he can't pronounce the R.

.

Diplomacy

I was born in 1968 in Batavia, New York, a small town southwest of Buffalo. I was a born disappointment. My parents put on a brave front, but as early as I can remember, my mother whispered about me to my father in the living room of our trailer, once my sister and I were tucked away in our tin box, tinderbox bedroom. "He's not, he's not . . . he's so, he's so . . . he's just, he just isn't . . . ." And then the endless questions: "How could he . . . ? Why wouldn't he . . . ? When will he . . . ?" and on and on.

I was small for my age with large prominent teeth, glasses and freckles. I liked to read war magazines. I knew all about all kinds of guns, tanks and bombs, about who won every battle since 1648. I was a terrible athlete and an obsessive nose picker. In grade school, I sat in the back of the class in worn, K-Mart size 6X military fatigues, my back hunched so my bony shoulder blades stuck out like razor blade wings. I shielded my gravity-defying front teeth with my nose-picking hand. I picked, licked and flicked and read books like *The Life and Times of a World War One General* and *How the Civil War Was Won* while the other kids pinched each other and giggled and filled out worksheets on reading comprehension or multiplication. I don't know if our teacher was afraid of me or impressed with my reading ability or if she was past caring, but she left me alone. Maybe she had a general policy on nonintervention. I can't remember her or anyone ever interceding on my behalf when the kids played Booger-Boy (a game in which I would hide and everyone else would set out to find me, rub my face in the pea gravel that had recently replaced the higher maintenance soccer field, call me a snotty little faggot and step on my fingers if I raised my head to scream). Booger-Boy was an excellent game, judging from the one or two times I played when somebody else was "it."

My father was a pathologically silent and chronically absent trucker. The subtext for his silence was months and years, a lifetime, of pent-up rage. My mother talked nonstop, criticizing, judging, speaking for my father, mocking him incessantly, but what I remember most about the feeling of home is the vacuum that was my father's presence. There was a meanness to his quiet. It was personal. He hated me, or at least that's how I interpreted his silences. I was a great one for interpreting. Always looking to make meaning out of the abyss. In those days, little was expected from fathers, so my father's endless withdrawal—broken only by occasional quiet rage-filled tremors and, here and there, a fist imprint on a bedroom or bathroom wall—was unremarkable. Several quaint illustrations from *Boy's Life*, picturing smiling, smartly uniformed, white boys squeezing fishing rods or building raccoon traps, hung in my room, covering the fist marks on the walls.

It wasn't up to me to find a way through to my father. In recent years, countless friends, university colleagues and shrinks have told me he must have set the tone long before I was born. How much of his mute rage was ancient, inherited, like scoliosis or colour blindness, and how much was a response to my mother's endless carping? I don't know, but too much fury in a coffin-shaped tin home is like too much hot or cold in a small shower stall. You leap and dance and writhe, but to no avail. I used to repeat in my head over and over until the words became a senseless rhythm, "I can't stand it. I can't stand it. I can't stand it." If I said it out loud, my mother said smugly, as if a child couldn't possibly understand the legitimate pain that was adult life, "How much can't you stand?"

Sometimes I tried talking to him as if he were a human being. "How was your day, Daddy?" "How do you like them Jets, Daddy?" "Tell me about the time you met Winston Churchill, Father." "Can I make you some ice-cold toast with fresh marmalade preserves, Papa?" I tried out these lines the way cowardly punks with nothing to do throw rocks at school windows late at night. They want a reaction, but they don't want to get caught. They are pretending to be someone else, but they crave the satisfying crash of dissolving glass, the automatic blast of the alarm, the sensual wail of a siren, the terror of a spotlight and then the pounding of their own sneakers on the hot asphalt and the feeling that their lungs are splitting because there is just never enough air when you are a rebel. That is the fantasy, but what is more likely to happen is that the rock, so deftly hurled, pings barely audibly off the school brick and falls back onto the playground. So it was with my efforts to get a response out of my father.

How did I become a supposedly functional, superficially suc-cessful person with many degrees and tenure? How, Dr. Freud, would ask, did I escape the web of doom that was laid out for me in childhood? The real question is, how did I create the impression of escaping? There is a catalogue of probable causes, but I'm not ashamed of what I am, just curious, the way some people are about other people. The one I am loath to bring up is Angela, or Dead Sib, as I lovingly refer to her. I don't want you to see my story in terms of cause and effect, but I don't want to hide anything, either. I've embraced the past and hurled it into the abyss. It's over, but here it is: Dead Sib is Mommy's little angel, was Brother's little crybaby punching bag. She was cute as a button with her big straight teeth and long, clown-curly hair. When she was alive, she was rumoured to have elicited smiles from one and all, even old tombstone face himself, Dad.

I was six and she was four when she ran out onto the road, the highway, actually. We lived practically in town, walking distance to the school, the FoodFare and Junior's Burgers and Fries, but the sloping driveway in front of our trailer spilled right onto the 307. "Watch your sister" was the last thing my mother said to me as she hurried us out the door so she could watch *The Edge of Night* in peace. "Watch your sister" to me and "Give Mommy a kiss" to Angela, and then we were outside in our yard where the grass was tall and going to seed and littered with remnants of life-sized, rusted-out old cars and smaller, fading Fisher-Price versions.

I don't remember what game we were playing—was it cat and mouse, explosion tag, double indemnity or our favourite, Get Dizzy?—but I do remember watching my sister. I watched her spin down the driveway, her arms out, her tangled honeycomb hair bobbing. I felt superior, smarter than her because her eyes were closed and she didn't know I could see her frilly yellow underpants flashing at me from under her jumper like her butt was a blooming carnation. I watched my sister whirl and derv right onto the 307 and I probably screamed when the white pickup truck swerved, screeched, but still picked her up and punted her chubby little princess-ness back onto our driveway. It was not like a movie. It did not happen in slow motion. Her body was not like a rag doll. The whole thing was loud, pulpy, in your face, sickening and jarring, not at all choreographed. Even her scream was deformed. It came out more like a hiccup than a protest. There was blood, I'm sure. I don't know how much pain she felt.

Then there was commotion—ambulances, false hope, despair—and always, even at a time when silence was the only acceptable response, always, the sound of my mother's accusations. She accused everyone—the truck driver, me, my father's bulky absence, the ambulance attendants, the doctors and nurses, the government and even the curve in the road. No one dared say, "Why did you let your kids play unattended by a busy highway?" maybe because in those days everyone sent their kids outside to play and let their dogs run loose and threw their burning cigarette butts out the passenger-side windows, even in school zones.

When I was working on my dissertation years later, I read that in the Middle Ages, parents left their toddlers home alone in huts with open fires burning in pits in the centre of each hut. Many a careless toddler went up in smoke or was charred for life. According to what I read, the firepit worked as a kind of man-made natural selection: a way of promoting the coveted attributes of diligence and caution and of discouraging whim. The highway is the trailer-trash version of the firepit. Those who aren't careful enough are weeded out as pre-schoolers, or as teenagers piled into trucks where they laugh and shriek and pass joints and Jack Daniel's whiskey bottles back and forth with their doomed compatriots. If they are lucky enough to grow up, they become truck drivers like my father, giant men who wheeze instead of speak, and live on diner Salisbury steak, mashed potatoes and cherry pie. They pop uppers to get them through the night runs and downers for when they pull in at the designated rest stops and heave themselves into their sardine-can bunks, which are the pride of their rigs.

So Angela (Dead Sib to me) was taken from us that day, but it was probably a case of sooner rather than later. Everything happens for a reason. When it's your time to go, it's your time to go. She's in a better place. God has a plan. She's with us in spirit. Watch your sister. Watch your sister. Watch your sister and on and on, as though life were a tanagram puzzle that, once solved, would yield an image so beautiful, so meaningful, so tangible that it would justify everything.

Angela and I shared a room, and after she got mushed, as often happens in such cases, at least those portrayed in arch, pastel, badly acted television dramas (of which my childhood was an even more hollow imitation), our bedroom became a shrine to her. For ages, nothing of hers was removed. The bottom two drawers of the dresser we shared remained filled with her neatly folded clothes. Her bed was like mine except the cheap headboard was painted pink and the sheets were a pasty lilac flannel. Everything I had was faded little boy blue. After Angela died, her bed was always made and somebody (could it have been Daddy Dearest?) even touched up the paint on the headboard where it had always been cracked and peeling. I have a memory of Angela, completely unverifiable, probably made up, of her picking at the paint on her head-board, making a game of collecting pink paint flakes under her pillow as a little secret treasure trove. I also remember (I think) that Angela liked to lick things. She was a frozen pole licker from way back and she also liked to gnaw on the occasional bedpost. If she'd ever grown up, I bet she would have had lead poisoning from all the paint chips she sucked back.

Anyway, enough about Dead Sib. I think of her now, when I think of her at all, as a dark cloud, sky dirt, like one of those cartoon dust storms that follows Pig-Pen or the Road Runner wherever he goes but never catches him. The fact is, she isn't here any more, but I am. That sounds childish, but it is what I would say to my mother if I ever talked to her about it.

In ninth grade, I got my government-issued braces and fought a losing battle to stretch my lips around them. They called me bird boy or bird brain, and later, just bird, I think because everything about me was fragile and frail except my mouth, which, with all those teeth and metal, jutted forward like a beak. I was not in the "in" crowd in high school, but there were fewer specific acts of violence against me than before. The other kids were too busy swaggering, drinking, flirting, fucking, flunking out and getting jobs at the Pay and Save. It should have been a good time for me. I maintained my good grades. I perfected my father's technique of not speaking except on pain of death to anyone and in particular not to my mom. I read a lot in high school, mostly military history, which distracted me best.

I read about the Civil War, the Boer War, the Great War, impending and current wars, Armageddon scenarios and any other war that was recorded in print. It was pre-Columbine, very pre-9/11. My interest in war was as harmless as a butter-fly collector's interest in wingspans or larvae gestation. I wasn't one of the Columbine killer types, despite my sullen, pimply isolation. I rarely dreamed about launching assaults on my gym class and almost never made priority hit lists. The lists I made were mental, no evidence, and only made in the most flimsy of idle daydreams. These dreams unravelled as soon as something, anything, material intervened. The odour of beans and bacon from the school cafeteria or the laugh track from the television down the hall at home was enough to snap me back. My reveries of mass destruction were not trances or states of transformation, but tiny annoyances or inconven-iences, like when you are trying to sleep and a fly is trying to escape your room through the sealed glass of a windowpane.

What fascinated me about war was not born of some juve-nile revenge. What I cared about were the details of war; the consequences. I shivered reading about soldiers battling lice and gangrene in the trenches of Europe. I sought out stories about poison arrow attacks on Wild West settlers. I knew all about burrowing, exploding shrapnel and what it felt like to have your flesh melt off along with your clothes in the eye of a nuclear explosion. My passion for the blood and guts of history was not academic. The treasured pages torn out of *Penthouse* or *Playboy* or cut-outs of the bikini-clad "girls" from the auto association calendar (prize possessions of my peers) didn't do it for me. I had to feign interest in the air-brushed nipples and navels, the balloon breasts and most-coveted splayed displays of what we boys called, as if to make it less fierce, *pussy*. The pouty-faced blondes with their empty expressions and unnaturally flowing hair only made me feel slightly green. But when I slept, I dreamed about exploding shrapnel bits lodged excruciatingly in eyes, groins, necks; the flesh-sizzling poetry of the atom bomb got me really excited.

Those were the dreams that made me smuggle my sheets and pajamas into the laundry to avoid inspections, accusations and hysterics. I didn't talk to my mother, and I didn't want to give her a topic to reconnect with me on, like the fact that I was potentially a sexual being. By this time most of her rants were mumbled and incoherent. She didn't know me well enough any more, or maybe she was going nuts, but the result was the same. I didn't want to risk her knowing anything about me. She thought I was mean and hopeless; lacking in potential to give her some minimal satisfaction. She didn't need to know I was a pervert even in my sleep.

So I was surviving high school more or less. If I hadn't been fifteen, maybe I would have been able to think ahead to a time when I would be free of my screaming meanie mother, my raging Buddha father, my zits, my aloneness, my utter stupefaction in the face of my peers and on and on, the usual teenage stuff. But I was fifteen, which meant suffocating in the interminable present. The only thing I had to hang on to was my obsession with pain. I had a picture of a mass grave, a World War II liberation photo, that I kept folded up in my jeans pocket. Whenever a girl or a teacher or a popular boy looked my way, I would touch the edge of the photo in my pocket and it gave me a charge. Other people had friends or drugs or family time. I had death and destruction and the glory of history. I was luckier than some.

I was surviving, but barely, which might be why, when a couple of boys from Junior Cadets decided to start an after-school Diplomacy Club, and they asked me to join on condition that the club could meet at my house, I agreed. Chad and Eric were Junior Cadets, something I might have been if it didn't require parental consent (which required an interaction with said parents) and money to shell out for a uniform. Eric and Chad were also skinny, snivelling, stammering losers. They were lousy at sports and shunned by the tier of teenagers who were cute and with it and actually having a life. The cool kids were vaguely flower power and anti war and very pro drugs. After all, it was 1973. The Diplomacy Club was kind of anti drugs and very pro war. Not so much Nam, but war in general, and we had a lot of nostalgia for the winnable wars of the past.

The Diplomacy Club met almost every day after school and the parts of the weekend that Chad and Eric weren't at cadets. Mainly what we did was play the game. In Diplomacy the board is a coloured map of pre-WWI Europe. There are no dice in the game, only negotiations on paper. The point of the game is to get enough allies to subdue the other player/countries and thus take over Europe. You do this by making and breaking promises. Like most good games, it's nasty, not nice. It takes about eight hours to finish a game and the more players, the better.

Mom was now used to me trooping in after school with Chad and Eric and the few other boys not cut out for football or hockey, but who were still angry enough to need a venue to hurt their friends (all in good fun). The members of the Diplomacy Club were briefed before entering the trailer: "Follow me. Don't speak when spoken to. Go directly to my room. Ignore all screeching and cajoling." My strategy with Mom worked. The first few times, she hollered things at us like, "Who are these hooligans?" and "This is my home!" But the troops kept their deadpan expressions (at least until the door was shut in my room and they started in on imitating my mom), so soon enough she stopped performing for them.

Diplomacy is a boys' game. It is strictly about abstract ambition, which, in its pure form, feels like the worst insatiable adolescent lust. Andrea McCrea was the only girl we allowed into the Diplomacy Club. She wasn't much of a girl— very pointy, very hostile, and she dressed only in army surplus fatigues. She was nothing like the *Sports Illustrated Calendar* images of women that dominated the locker walls of the other members of the club or the dirty magazine images they used to stock their dreams. Andrea's lack of authentic girlishness made the rest of us feel cocky around her. She was a girl, but she didn't scare us, not really. We would toss her on Dead Sib's bed and tickle her or pinch her until she agreed to do things for us: sneak past Mom and get us Kool-Aid from the kitchen; put the game away when it was over; make out with the picture of Paul McCartney, which we discovered in her knapsack. Andrea took our teasing stoically as the price she had to pay for being a girl in a boys' club. She never complained about it or about our tacit pact never to let her win the game. We could do that because in order to win at Diplomacy you need to form allegiances. We knew unconsciously that to let Andrea win would be to unleash unbearable humiliation on ourselves as future men. Andrea was almost always the first player eliminated, and when she was, she would crumple her strategy sheets, flick her dirty, dirty blonde hair out of her eyes and laugh as though she loved to lose. Chad or one of the other boys would give her a shove off my bed where the players sat and she would go and sit on Dead Sib's bed and bite her nails and give me advice on how to outmanoeuvre the other guys.

I think I was nice to her, or at least not cruel. I don't remember calling her embarrassingly stupid nicknames like *wench* or asking her horrible questions like, "How come your zits are bigger than your tits?" like some of the other boys did.

Andrea was included in the Diplomacy Club, we told ourselves, because everyone knows that the game works best with more players, but really it was because we needed someone whose social status was even lower than ours. If I had asked myself, "What did I want from Andrea?" I wouldn't have known the answer and still don't know it now. Did I want her to be my girlfriend? Did I want her to detonate and spatter herself on us boys, her bones shattered into shrapnel, smart shrapnel, like smart bombs, that could find an eye or a lung or a heart? Did I want her to be what I think she wanted to be, a guy like the rest of us? It was crazy that she wanted to be us: wormy, pathetic, basically ordinary boys that we were. I don't know what I wanted from Andrea, only that I wanted something and that her wanting to be like us made our disdain for her justifiable somehow.

One night around ten o'clock, the game was almost over. Chad had been knocked out early and Andrea had managed to consolidate most of Western Europe and was closing in on the UK. Even with Eric and me joining forces, it seemed inevitable that Andrea would win. Her face was red with concentration and she fluttered somehow from her cross-legged position on the bed. Chad was lying on Dead Sib's bed with his face in a *Penthouse* centrefold. I was feeling miffed at Chad because it seemed like he'd lost on purpose. "Chad, would you rather sniff airbrushed pussy than take over Europe?" I asked. "You're a pretty sick puppy."

"It's real, Booger Boy. Does that scare you?" he said, shoving the picture at me. This kicked off a round of calling each other fags, something we did like breathing, it happened so often and so effortlessly. We even included Andrea—I could get some kind of smile out of her by calling her The Dairy Queen Hot Fudge Boy—but I was annoyed that Chad didn't seem to want to finish the game. "*Penthouse* won't get you through life," I told him.

"Play your little game," he said, as if Diplomacy was one of many trivial pastimes and not the fundamental force in our lives.

Eric laughed when Chad mocked the game, like for a long time he and Chad had both known that salivating over sexy pictures was far more important than ruling early twentieth-century Europe.

Andrea said, "Just because I'm winning. Come on. Let's finish the game."

But Eric started flicking the coloured board pieces around, playing with them like tiddlywinks, and then he flipped the board. It was my chance to stand up for fair play, to tell Chad and Eric off or kick them out of the club, but that would have meant taking Andrea's side. She had become very still on her corner of the bed. The redness of her face had spread to the rims of her eyes so they looked like little gerbil eyes and she added to the effect by silently grinding her teeth so that there was a rhythmic hollow appearing and disappearing in her cheek. I could have stood up for her, but I was training for war, not a good citizen award, and, besides, she had been beating me too. I told Andrea to get her big smelly feet and her bony ass off my bed. "I won't be able to sleep with the stench of you," I told her.

She jumped up like she was going to fight me. But the three of us jumped up too. We stood there facing off, me and my two loyal buddies and Andrea, the freak of the world, until she backed down, grabbed her sweater and shoes, and took off.

After that, Andrea was out of the club. We didn't see her

much. I heard she joined the Hare Krishnas instead of finishing high school. Someone had seen her hanging around the Buffalo airport in a hippie skirt and those cheap Indian sandals. She'd shaved her head and rumour was, she was high as Mount Rushmore most of the time. After Andrea dropped out, instead of playing Diplomacy, the members of the club hung around my room, talking about how we'd like to get Andrea McCrea. Our disdain for her was the glue that kept us from getting completely sick of each other and drifting into random violence or mute despair.

A few weeks before senior prom, we stumbled across Andrea when I met Chad and Eric uptown on the way home from their cadets meeting. They had their buzz cuts and their shiny boots and their thick green uniforms to make them feel big. I had Chad and Eric to make me feel connected. Andrea had her bald head, her tin can, her crappy sandals, her madras clothes, her red eyes and her chanting to get her through. She stood outside the bus depot, saving souls and begging for nickels. We hadn't seen her for almost two years. We had demonized her for so long and with such intensity that when we actually saw her, we fell over each other to be nice to her.

"Hey Andrea, how's it hangin'?"

"Hare Krishna, brothers."

"Harry fuckin' Krishna, Andrea," Chad said. Now that he was seventeen and almost a soldier, he was developing leadership qualities.

Andrea smiled this serene, sleep-deprived smile. She looked scary. Sick, even. Pathetic. She looked Biafran. We should have been inspired to pity, or at least indifference. But she had never been one of us, not really. Probably Chad hated her because she was the one girl who had ever tried to be his friend. She reminded him that the women of his dreams would never give him a backwards glance. Eric hated her because she'd had the nerve to almost beat him at Diplomacy; that really galled him, but mainly he hated her because we all did. Eric was the kind of guy who, if he saw a group of people stoning Jesus Christ or anyone else, he'd get down on his knees and find the biggest rock to throw. Chad was the leader, which made him dangerous in one way, but Eric was all joiner, which was worse.

I can't say that I hated her, but even in her frail, crazy, Hare Krishna state, even with her emaciated cheeks, her barely there breasts and her boyish hips, she was someone special to me. She had that thing, even if just barely, even if pathetically and laughably, that is known today as girl power. She had that thing, and I wanted it for myself.

We sat down with her outside the bus depot. It was chilly outside, so Chad took off his cadet jacket and hung it over her bone-rack shoulders. We talked about school, about our plans for after we graduated (Chad and Eric were enlisting, I was hoping for a college scholarship so I wouldn't have to go with them). Andrea's future had already arrived and we didn't discuss it.

Andrea said she should be getting back to the hostel. She had to turn in the tin can with its handful of coins by midnight, but Chad persuaded her that there was no harm in joining us for just one session of the Diplomacy Club. For the good old days. We joked about what kids we were to take winning so seriously. I don't know why she agreed to come home with us, but Andrea wasn't exactly what you would call astute. Maybe she liked showing off her new image of vulnerability with her sleep-deprived cow eyes, her concentration-camp cheekbones and her rattling tin can. Maybe she was weak or stupid or still wanted love or maybe she thought she could convert us. Or maybe she just wanted what was rightfully hers—the chance to finish that aborted Diplomacy game and beat us all.

It wasn't hard to persuade her to come to the trailer with us. It was harder when we were there to get her to lie still on Dead Sib's pristine pink sheets. We had to put a rag in her mouth and then we pulled her madras skirt up over her head so she was just a bony cunt with legs. It was a shock how white her thighs were. That little snarl of light brown pubic hair meant she wasn't a kid. She thrashed around a little and dug her fingertips (her nails were chewed down, as they had always been) into my arm where I held her while Chad gave her what Eric called (snicker, snicker) fresh, raw meat. Andrea's lower half was almost comical, like one of those underground x-rated cartoon drawings that were all the rage back then. Her stick legs twitched pathetically, but soon she stopped fighting and stopped making the choking sounds. Chad was fast and professional. A few months before, as an early grad present, his dad had bought him an hour with a prostitute, so he was experienced. Chad was on and off her, zipped and unzipped in the time it takes to chug half a bottle of beer.

Chad took over holding her arms and dared me and Eric to take our turns. We were scared shitless. We sat Andrea up and got out some beers I'd stolen from my dad and saved under the bed for a special occasion. Everyone needed a beer. With the first few sips, I felt a little warm inside, like there was a way to carry on with the day. Like I hadn't just blinked and taken the exit to hell rather than a nice college scholarship out of this jackass town. I was still half-heartedly holding Andrea, so I curled up next to her with my arm around her. I took the rag out of her mouth, smoothed down her skirt and stroked the dents on both sides of her bald head. She slumped up against me and I fed her sips from my beer. Eric was pacing back and forth, freaking out. He had lost his moment. The spontaneity was gone and now he was probably going to go overseas and get his legs blown off without ever getting laid.

Chad said, "Relax, man, she wants you too. Right, Kojak?" Andrea clawed at me like a cat at the vet. I fed her more beer and stroked her and, mysteriously, she trusted me, even though I didn't stick up for her or protect her. I didn't do anything right. I sat next to her, feeding her sips of beer out of cowardice more than compassion. The beer made her calmer and after a while, I said, "Come on, let's play Diplomacy. That's why we're here, isn't it?"

This was something I'd said many evenings of the Diplomacy Club when we were spinning our wheels, bragging or arguing or otherwise not focussing. Andrea started with France and Scandinavia and I had Russia and England. Without ever discussing it or questioning it, Andrea and I played like partners; we got all the best countries, and wiped out Chad and Eric in record time. Chad was gallant, as though none of us had a past together, not even a recent past, and as though it really was only a game. Eric was less cool. He was falling apart, frothing and mumbling, making stupid, suicide plays. Andrea was slow and clumsy at first. I had to move her pieces for her, but quickly her awkwardness turned into a contagious giddiness. A half hour into the game, Andrea and I were giggling intolerably at each conquest. She said things like "the lady emergeth victorious" and I murmured, fawned and demurred. In the end, the shame in the room was acted out only by Eric, whose lips quivered when he saw that losing was inevitable. He rubbed his eyes furiously to keep the tears leaking from his eyes. Chad was disgusted with Eric, and Eric's humiliation overshadowed Andrea's surprise emergence as a force in the game.

You might think that I joined first with the boys and then with Andrea that night as a wormy way of always staying on the winning side. I can't defend against that accusation. But that night, Andrea and I were merged not by choice or by force of will, but by the facts of where we were and what I had let happen to her. It was the same way when Dead Sib died. She wasn't there any more, but I was. The cloud of pink dust that was all that was left of her attached to me like gum in the roots of my hair. It was my job to live out what was left of her, to wear her corpse like a necklace and obey her whispered commands to live as she should have lived.

Most people think Eric was killed in Vietnam. Actually, he was killed in a scooter accident in Tokyo on his first leave. I don't know if he killed anyone first. Chad made it back from Vietnam in one piece and now had that insane war as the presumed cause of all his psychic grief. He became a peace activist and later a real estate tycoon. He was one of the big winners in that swamp in Florida development. He got out early, pretty much unscathed, I heard.

I won my scholarship and started college in the fall. I entered academic life like I was entering a monastery. I went straight through from first year to finishing my PhD in history (specializing in mediaeval childhood) in six years. By then the draft was over, though the only universities hiring mediaevalists were in obscure Canadian cities, so now I'm stuck in one. I've been in Canada for over twenty years. I was married for five of those years and have a son. My parents died without knowing their grandson or getting over their disappointment in me. On my occasional visits home while I was in college and my mom was giving way to emphysema, I sometimes hinted that my childhood had been less than idyllic. "All water under the bridge," I wanted to say, once she admitted the worst of it. But she wouldn't let me start in on it. She would cut me off by making her eyes fill up with tears and gargling in her oxygen-starved way about herself: "I was grieving then, son. Grieving my little angel. Grief is like a blood blister. You swell up with pain and there's nothing else."

After the game, we walked Andrea back to the bus depot. I kept my arm around her like I had all through the game, even though my muscles were aching. She wanted me close to her and I wanted myself separate from Chad and Eric. Eric did some Laugh-In routine as we walked that had Chad laughing. At the doors to the depot, we said "Goodbye" and "See you around" and "Next time, it's my turn to take over the world," but I think we all knew what a pile of horseshit we were spewing. There was no next time.

I still said hi to Eric and Chad in the few months I saw them around town before they shipped out and before I went off to college, but whatever had masqueraded as friendship between us had decisively fled. I might have seen Andrea and even dated her if I'd made the effort. Maybe she would have remembered me as the guy who rescued her from the clutches of the Hare Krishnas. Instead, whenever I was leaving town or coming home to visit, I used the far door at the bus depot and skulked in or out as fast as possible. When I heard the rattle of a tin cup and that unmistakable chant, I didn't look up.

Before and After

Everyone's life has a before and after point; innocence gained or lost; God found or found ridiculous. I can't remember mine. Maybe it happened at Goosey Goosey Gander nursery school, the day my mom didn't show up to pick me up because there was black ice and she grew up in Los Angeles so she didn't know how to drive on black ice, and she'd rolled the orange Volkswagon van. It was strange waiting in a room full of children's things—easels, a play kitchen, dress-up clothes and nap mats—with no other children there. Everything was carefully put away for the next day. It didn't matter, because I knew that my job then was to wait and not to play. I knew it would be my fault if I was playing greedily and *something* happened to my mom. Maybe it happened that day, but my mom did come eventually and we rode home in a taxi together and I was allowed to sit on her lap and hear the story of the accident. So it probably wasn't that day.

Jeremy Jebbings, a wild-haired blond boy who sat behind me in grade two, liked to sharpen pencils until they were deadly weapons and then do acupuncture experiments on the hollow space between my scrawny shoulder blades. I would squirm and whisper, "Ow, cut it out, Jeremy. Owww." It didn't occur to me to turn him in. The poking seemed just like one of those things you have to endure when you are old enough to go to school. I did sometimes worry that the lead from the pencils would poison my blood and kill me, but I was a shy kid. One day, Jeremy came to school with a new pencil sharpener. It was blue and shaped like a car. He showed it to me when they were standing up for "Oh Canada." He held it out like an offering: "Look, Mitzy, vroom vroom."

I took a quick glance and then pretended I hadn't heard him. Nothing about Jeremy Jebbings made sense to me. The new pencil sharpener proved more effective than the last. We were correcting spelling tests from the day before when he got me for the first time. It was my turn to offer the class the correct spelling for the word "modern." At that moment, he got me, square in the back. I shot straight up, banged my knees on the bottom of my desk and audibly yelped, "Holy fuck!" There was a sound all around me like a wave crashing or an animal roaring. I looked at Miss Thurstead and saw that even she was laughing. She was wiping her eyes, she was laughing so hard. She couldn't speak and was reduced to making hand gestures to indicate to the class that they should settle down. The thirty seconds or so it took for her to gain her composure was one of those before and after points for her.

At home, the F word functioned like most people use *um*. There was the fucking government, the fucking kids, Jesus Christ on a fucking crutch. And the one I loved because I loved birds: fuck a duck. Between Mom and my brother,

Nicky, the word *fuck* had been elevated to an art form. It was a kind of blasphemy for either one of them to utter more than two sentences without including *fuck* in some innovative way. If they couldn't be innovative, they would go for quantity in lieu of quality. But I had learned quickly that swearing was not something you did at school. Swearing was one of the private rituals, like common limericks or recipes that made your family special. In my house, we used *fuck* the way some families use pet names or nicknames.

I loved Miss Thurstead but I was terribly disappointed in her lack of outrage at my filthy mouth. I wanted her to punish me, not laugh at me. I needed a civilized punishment, not a brutal one. I should be sent to the principal's office or made to stand out in the hallway until recess. I needed to believe that in the outside world, people knew how to behave and how to follow the rules. It wasn't right for home and school to coincide in an anarchy of manners. It wasn't right for grade two teachers to laugh until their faces were red and their breasts were heaving.

When Miss Thurstead could talk again, she called Jeremy Jebbings up to her desk and they whispered to each other for a few minutes. Then she confiscated his new pencil sharpener and asked me to get back to spelling "modern." All the rest of the day, Jeremy sat behind me, jabbing me with his finger.

After grade two, Jeremy transferred to a different school and soon after I moved away. I hadn't thought about him much except to wonder if he cheated when he marked his own spelling tests the way I did. We had both been good spellers and I found it impossible to write "14/15" at the top of my page when adding an "l" or crossing out an "e" would allow me to write "15/15." When I did think about him years later, it occurred to me that maybe the pencil-sharpening torture was his way of showing affection. Or maybe not.

There was one day, when I was nine or ten, after we'd moved to rural Vancouver Island, I was cutting through my neighbour's yard. I liked to run wherever I went and I was fairly flying along when I looked at the fir tree between the porch and the front walk. Suddenly I knew that I was a believer. There is a God. The tree proved it by the miracle of its very ordinary treeishness. It was an ecstatic moment. For months, every time I ran through the yard to play with Katya, the mean little girl who lived in the next house and tortured ants and spiders, I just had to look quickly at the tree and I could feel what I knew was perfect truth. But we moved again, and I tried looking at other trees and some were breathtaking and some were ordinary, but none were pure simple unadulterated truth. And now I remember knowing about God, but I don't feel what I knew then. I even went back and visited and the tree is still there—it's taller than the house now, healthy and stoical—but it is just a tree and I don't know anything, so maybe that wasn't my moment.

I heard that when Jeremy Jebbings was sixteen, he got drunk and dived head-first into an empty swimming pool. He survived, but was paralyzed from the neck down. That's one way to understand before and after.

They Eat Their Young

Pervert. Scooter victim. Bacterial meningitis. ADD. Bully. Less than average grades. Broken home. Sibling torture. Poverty. No valentines. Head injury. Vocational school. Low self-esteem. Delusional. Bad manners. Video game addict. No friends. Wrong friends. Prettier friends. Uglier friends. Appendicitis. Dyslexia. Klutz. Fatty. Zit-face. Sniveller. Whiner. Weirdo. Ordinary Joe. Conformist. Nonconformist. Vandalizer. Shoplifter. Nose picker. Terrorist. Can't read. Won't read. Special child. Difficult child. Stepchild. Ju-V-D. Too short. Too tall. Failure. Loser. Freak.

A child who isn't vigilantly watched over, nudged and nurtured, could become any of the above. But none of the parents huddled outside Very Pleasant Elementary School are thinking about these horrors. Instead they are behaving proactively; positively. All are doing whatever it takes to give their children the best chance. Jocelyn Green, mother of three children (Zak, Jilly and Dylan), all three born at home, Zak at a birthing bash potluck that included twenty-five guests and a vat of vegetarian chili (the smell of chili still makes Jocelyn retch), Jilly in the bathtub with a smaller cheering committee—the midwife, Dan and three-year-old Zak screaming that he needed to take a bath with Mommy—and then Dylan, with only Dan and the midwife. After twelve hours of heated debate about going to the hospital, Dylan emerged, nine and a half pounds, bum first. Dan said that his first gesture was to crap on the world before he'd even set eyes on it.

Jocelyn is nervous about the night ahead of shivering jocularity with these other parents. Gail is the only one Jocelyn knows well enough to consider a friend. The others are random acquaintances linked only by the school and their kids who are or will be thrown together for the next six years. The good thing is that Jocelyn gets a night off midnight duty with two-year-old Dylan, and maybe, just maybe, that will be all he needs to give up nursing. Not that she is against nursing a two-year-old. She believes in child-led feeding as well as learning, but it is exhausting feeding a thirty-pound kid who can sing "O Canada" in French. Tonight she is here for Jilly who is starting grade one in September. Registration for Very Pleasant's "Other" education program begins at eight a.m. tomorrow and, like the other would-be Other parents, Jocelyn will stay here all night so that she can ensure Jilly a spot. She did the same thing three years ago when Zak was starting grade one. It was that or home schooling. She will chat up the newbie parents, try to make them feel comfortable and welcome. They will be reassured to see that she is back for her second child. Everyone gathered on the steps here in the mid-February deep freeze agrees that the Other Ed. program is the best chance for their children to survive public education and life in the big, brutal world. There is a sense of camaraderie and a party atmosphere that reminds Jocelyn of the time she was sixteen and waited in line all night for Grateful Dead tickets. Everyone knew their place in line and so there was no point in feeling competitive or hostile to those in front, who might very well get the last tickets. Also, as fellow Dead Heads, they were united in their belief that the sacrifice of an all-nighter was not only worthwhile, but what any thinking person would do.

Every year, the lineup starts earlier. Years ago, parents would arrive at seven or seven-thirty the morning of registration. Whoever arrived first would feel silly, like an overinvolved parent, but inevitably there would be some families put on waiting lists and encouraged to register their children in the equally fine Regular program "just in case." The next year, the diehards would be there even earlier.

It's only eight in the evening, twelve hours before registration officially begins, and already there are half a dozen parents huddled on the steps. Dave Myers has been circling the school in his SUV on the half hour. Each time he passes the front of the school, he slows down to count the number of parents on the steps. He is on his cellphone the whole time to his wife, Marnie. When the numbers are close to maximum, he will go home for supplies and head over to the school. He and Marnie have a daughter going into grade four (already in the program) and a son in kindergarten they will be fighting for tonight.

On this pass, Gail Janowitch, the chair of the Parent Council, waves to him. She is holding forth to the group, but it's okay that Dave can't hear her. He knows what she's telling them because he was on the committee that came up with the registration guidelines: "Bathroom breaks of no longer than ten minutes are allowed without forfeiting your place in line. Surrogate spot holders are allowed (only one child per surrogate). Surrogate must arrive before the parent leaves or the spot is forfeited. Spots are nontransferable. Parents will sign the list on the door in the order in which they arrive. No bribery. The school division and the Parent Council will not be responsible for any injury or death incurred due to waiting all night in the freezing cold. Parent Council volunteers will provide coffee, doughnuts and extra blankets. Depending on the wind chill and the discretion of the caretaker, parents may be allowed to wait in the gym during the night."

As Gail talks, the parents shuffle their feet, nudge each other and whisper rebellious remarks. Gail's chummy "here we go again" attitude and her "I know how important your children are to you; I'm a mother too" intro is embarrassing. Jocelyn feels like a teenager herself, hanging around with the cool kids on the school steps as though she's one of the crowd. She puts her gloved hand up to her face and takes an imaginary drag on an imaginary cigarette. She hasn't smoked since she was a teenager. She blows pretend smoke into the chilly February night air. Unlike real junior high, no one jeers at her or even notices her gesture.

"Quite the riot act," George Clark, so far the lone male in the group, whispers to Liz Anderson, a tight-faced sleep-deprived over-earnest first-timer who wears a black trench coat and unnaturally auburn hair as remnants of her once trendy youth.

"Do you think they'll provide porta-potties?" she shoots back, and George can't tell if she's joking or really distraught about the ten-minute bathroom rule. He says he's only here because his wife insisted. "When I was a kid, you went to the neighbourhood school. There was no special program, no French immersion, no Other Ed., no back-to-basics movements." But his wife, Andrea, said it was Very Pleasant's Other program or Ravenscourt, the snooty boys' school that now takes girls too and costs ten grand a year regardless of gender. George says his daughter, Jamie, is a tough little bugger, a lot like her dad, who will land on her feet regardless of where she goes to school, but an all-nighter with a bunch of beautiful women is better than ten grand a year.

George has managed to whisper all this to Liz while Gail is still talking.

"Can you believe this is the best system they can come up with?" Jocelyn is saying, even though she had planned to say only warm, community-building things.

"Yeah, it scares me too," George says, but he is speaking to Liz, not Jocelyn, agreeing with something Liz said.

Jocelyn senses George's dismissal of her and is moved to engage Gail as an ally. Jocelyn, like Gail, knows her way around. She has gone on field trips, cut out construction-paper shadow children, rinsed old milk cartons and sat on Parent Council meetings with Gail. They are practically friends. They know each other's phone numbers by heart, but, more importantly, they have made the Other program their own. They are the gatekeepers to the Other community. Staying up all night on the steps of the school may get your child registered in the program, but only when people like Gail and Jocelyn remember your phone number and call you at eleven-thirty when they need hot dog buns picked up from Price Cutters for the hot dog lunch that starts at twelve noon, only then are you a full-fledged member of the school community.

Gail finishes her spiel and people have asked her to repeat the parts they didn't hear and someone, George, asks the inevitable yearly question, "What about starting a committee to recommend a less insane, more equitable process of registration?"

Gail jokes, "We've talked about it a lot, but with our consensus approach, some of those babies conceived at these all-nighters will have long since graduated before we agree on a new approach."

When there is a lull in the talk and laughter, Jocelyn says, "Thanks for being here, Gail, when we all know you've already done your time." She adds for the benefit of the newbies, "Gail has two children in the program and a daughter in the Junior High Other program at Sagetory Junior High."

There is a murmur of respect and appreciation.

"If I look cheerful, it's because I'm registering my youngest," Gail says. "This is the last time I have to do this."

Sometime later, when Dave and three or four mothers have joined them, and when it seems as though the cold is really settling in, an enormously tall woman appears on the sidewalk, pushing a wheelbarrow and dragging two young boys, both in black and yellow snowmobile suits. The giraffe woman is so tall that she must bend almost in half to reach the handles of the wheelbarrow. The boys are pushing each other into the snowbanks as an inept method of keeping warm rather than helping with the wheelbarrow, which is laden with a mountain of goods, including what appears to be a dead baby, eyes crammed shut, face in a rigor mortis grimace and body rod-like inside its puffed-up baby bunting. All of a sudden she bellows, "Spencer! Braxton! Get your lazy butts over here and push."

The two boys jump to attention, but then squabble over one handle of the wheelbarrow. "Mom, get him off. I got here first," one insists.

"No me," says the other, "no me," and again and again, "no me!" at ever increasing pitch.

The woman is Kim, a parent with children in the Regular program. She is a constant presence in the school, volunteering, attending Parent Council and working in the school lunch program. Jocelyn knows the kids call her the Lunch Program Nazi because she likes to pick on smaller kids and invent crises to solve with the larger ones. "Zak, you must have dislocated your shoulder jumping off that swing. Let me pop it back into place for you," she once offered and Zak had broken the school's cardinal rule and left the school grounds at a run. He tried to run home, but only made it to the killer crosswalk at Corydon (killer because its white paint and flashing lights give the illusion that cars will stop when children try to cross), when Jocelyn, who had been called by the lunch program chief, caught up with him. Another time, Dale Allens was stung by a wasp on the playground and started to cry and Kim called him a first-rate drama queen. Then his wrist swelled up like a gourd and Miss Applebee, the French teacher who herself was allergic to almost everything in the world, drove him to the hospital while the principal tried to get through to his mother on the phone. Now he has an EpiPen he has to wear all the time and on half the nice days, they won't let him go outside at all, but it was worth it because even at eight years old, he could see how much Kim was sweating when he was ballooning. Later, when she told the story, Kim ended it with, "I saved Dale Allens's life, but does he even say thank you, ma'am? No sir." Nor did it stop Dale's older brother, Seth Allens, and his gang of junior high toughs from egging Kim's house every Hallowe'en and some other nights too.

Kim is nearing the school steps now and the parents are silent. The parents step back a little as Kim approaches. She looks capable of anything. They are in an unfamiliar place and the only light is the orange from the street lamps. Jocelyn doesn't like Kim, and likes her even less for pulling this stunt. Kim and her Regular parent cohorts often stand on the street during school hours, spitting distance from school property, smoking cigarettes and talking about the oh-so-special Dresden china *Other* kids and their oh-so-precious parents.

If Kim is part of this all-night affair, surely someone has made a mistake, Jocelyn thinks. Either the parents huddled on the school steps have or Kim has. Jocelyn can't believe Kim wants Braxton, her son who is starting grade one with a vocabulary of two ungrammatical words ("no me"), to join the Other program, but maybe she is in the process of some kind of conversion. Jocelyn must do something to keep the rest of the parents from panicking, packing up their blankets and thermoses and bolting. It's up to Jocelyn to break the ice because Gail won't speak to Kim. Gail hasn't spoken to Kim for five years, not since Arthur, Gail's second oldest, was kicked out of the lunch program for allegedly smearing peanut butter on the lunchroom table. Arthur had denied everything. Kim had written in her report, "Peanut butter is not allowed in the school. It's a dangerous substance (sic). But there was Arthur, rubbing it into the table." Gail had called the principal and explained that it was almond butter, but the principal had refused to see the distinction.

"Kim, how are you?" Jocelyn says and can feel herself smiling with rigid good will.

Kim pretends Jocelyn is fresh dogshit on the school steps, but Jocelyn tries again anyway.

"So you're registering Braxton then? The sign-up sheet is right here on the door."

Kim scowls and straightens up, swatting each of her boys

off the wheelbarrow and into the snow. Seeing Kim face-to-face is like a sasquatch sighting. Kim says, "Regular's good enough for Spencer. It's good enough for Braxton too. We're not Other. We're Regular. Always been."

There is a silent release of breath and tension. The group can continue to wait, freeze, bond, and, in the morning, start their kids off right. It turns out the baby isn't dead. It starts to stir and grumble, and from close up, they can see the frost around its mouth is wet from its breathing. Kim picks it up and reveals the real treasures in her wheelbarrow. She has a selection of hand warmers, the kind in plastic sacks that you smack with a rock or against a brick corner of a building and then they release a few hours of heat. She also has several bags of salt and vinegar potato chips and some cans of Safeway Select imitation Sprite.

They all look up at Kim holding the baby and lie about how adorable he seems. Braxton and Spencer roll around in the snow like arctic pro wrestlers. Kim grimaces down at the newbies and scowls at Jocelyn and Gail. Everyone but Gail buys something, and Dave buys a round of soft drinks for the house. They are glad when the transactions are complete and Kim and her brood trundle off in search of new adventures.

Around nine-thirty, the caretaker, Mr. Rauh, opens the door and invites everyone inside for the night. The cheer that goes up is feeble only because the grim effects of freezing ears, fingers, toes and lips will take a good hour to wear off. Anita Heinrichs, a youngish mother with a dime-sized hole in one earlobe, has already stormed off, announcing that she is too f-ing cold to stand here all night and that she will be suing the school (presumably for discrimination against parents who only own suede jackets and, like teenage girls, refuse the humiliation of wearing hats).

Inside, the parents spread out in the gym, most lucking out with a two-by-four gym mat all to themselves. Jocelyn puts her mat near Liz's along the back wall near the basketball hoop, and George hones in close to Liz. Throughout the gym there are little clusters of three or four parents and, here and there, the odd single. Dave is alone at the centre, stretched out on his back, eyes towards the ceiling beams. He refuses a blanket and his only item of comfort is his cellphone which is losing power and beeping at odd intervals. Whenever it beeps, he twitches awake and pats it like a sick child. The lay of parents on the gym floor reminds Jocelyn of natural formations kids fall into on the playground at recess. Most kids draw and are drawn to the kids most like them, but some are north and south magnets, repelling everyone. The doors to the gym are open and behind the din of conversation is the sound of Mr. Rauh's floor polisher in the hallway.

Outside the gym door, Mr. Rauh stops and leans in. "You tell me if you need anything," he says. Then he points at Jocelyn and says, "That one, she's a troublemaker. You watch out for her."

Jocelyn blushes but is happy that Mr. Rauh singles her out. The children like Mr. Rauh and the parents too find him reassuring and warm. The name *caretaker* suits him. Jocelyn tells George and Liz that Mr. Rauh has been the night caretaker in the school for almost thirty years.

"He's such a nice man," Jocelyn says, though the generalization is inadequate. Who is this person who cleans up their children's chalk marks, pee stains, mud and slush streaks and even their vomit? He is an immigrant from eastern Europe and there are rumours that he was an important scientist there after the war. Maybe he was a political dissident. Maybe he was persecuted for being Jewish or knowledgeable or ignorant. Maybe he was a petty thief or a revolutionary. Maybe he was forced to flee and leave his family behind. Perhaps he lived for weeks or months in tents or, if he was lucky, in a gym like this one as he waited for permission to come to North America. In that case, Jocelyn thinks, the building that warehoused Mr. Rauh would have been similar to Very Pleasant Elementary, square, plain, one storey, with metal bars on the lower windows. One difference would have been the barbed wire fence surrounding it and the tired, grey soldiers with rifles whose job was to keep Mr. Rauh and the other outsiders in.

It's late, some time between midnight and four a.m., when the hours of the night are weighted in favour of dying over living. Jocelyn squirms on her gym mat. She tries all possible sleeping positions: the foetal position, the traditional birthing position (back flat, knees bent) and even stretching out so her head and legs hang over the end of the mat against the gritty, cold gym floor, but it feels wrong, ungainly, to break the boundaries of the rectangular blue mat, and the floor is so unwelcoming that she must contain herself on the dingy slab that is covered in the shiny, unnatural blue plastic common to gym mats in schools and community clubs all over the world. It's dark now in the gym, except for the light from the hallway that comes through the cracks in the doors. Most people are sleeping or pretending to sleep. Jocelyn thinks of herself as shipwrecked on her little blue island, surrounded by other would-be survivors on their own blue remnants of salvation. She is lonely in a way she hasn't felt since before she met Dan and certainly not since they had Zak. She remembers the feeling of life-defying loneliness that had a stranglehold on her and caused her to do things she still regretted from about age thirteen until she met Dan and moved in with him. The feeling is one part terror, one part apathy and another part hate. She survived those years by making up mottos to herself like "Say yes to drugs." She lived on cigarettes, potato chips and most of all toking—she remembers the way the first toke ripped through her lungs like fire and how the second or third one made all other feelings blurry, bearable and just plain silly. She is horrified now at how she wasted her adolescence, didn't apply herself, didn't learn anything, but if one of the other parents right now whispers in her ear, does she want to go into the can and get high, she isn't sure she could say no. She listens to her heartbeat and the breathing of the others and tries to ground herself by thinking of the people in the world she loves and is loved by—Dan, Zak, Jilly and Dylan—but they aren't here with her in the gym and she is unable to conjure them in convincing detail. All around her is the tide of indifferent strangers and acquaintances.

Jocelyn manages to sleep for a while and the night creeps towards morning. At one point she is nudged awake and offered a swig from a bottle of vodka. It's Gail, who has been reborn as a teenage hoodlum making a scene at a party. She slurs her words and sways, having given up respecting personal space or other arbitrary, sobriety-imposed boundaries. Her voice is clumsy and loud and Jocelyn hopes for Gail's sake that Gail is the kind of drunk who is blessed with blackouts so she will never have to reconcile her excellent mother, Parent Council chair self with this drunken cartoon version.

"Come on, Joc. Help me celebrate. This is the last all-nighter. Last kid. I get the days to myself. Help me celebrate."

"I'm sleeping, Gail. Sorry."

"Party Poop."

Most people are awake now. Gail goes around, offering her mickey to everyone and many take her up on it.

There is laughter and back-slapping and most everyone has become old friends. Everyone except Dave, who remains passed out in the centre of the gym, and Jocelyn, who has never had a stomach for hard liquor. Jocelyn is embarrassed at her inability to, in Gail's words, *have some fun*, as she watches her peers get lubricated.

"Sorry," she says when Gail offers her the bottle for the fourth time. "Not my drug of choice." She means to be light, non-judgmental, in her refusal, but Gail is too hammered to catch the nuance.

"It's not crack, Honey; it's mother's milk," she says, shoving the bottle at Jocelyn again.

"Back off," Jocelyn hisses, and Gail mutters a slur of insults, but finally staggers over to join the parents who are organizing a game of Spin the Bottle in the far corner of the gym.

Somehow Jocelyn falls asleep again. Near morning she is awakened to the sound of Gail cursing and retching in the small washroom next to the gym. Jocelyn opens her eyes to see Liz and George groping each other from their twin mats in the dawn's early light. They did not brashly pile the mats together, so their groping involves a lot of stretching and reaching.

Jocelyn shuts her eyes again and keeps them closed until around six o'clock when most of the parents are awake. In the daylight, the only trace of the middle-of-the-night partying is the slight smell of vomit and the look of suffering on Gail's puffed face. Liz and George have become strangers again and Jocelyn and most of the parents are cheerful, knowing their children will certainly have spots in the Other program (there are sixteen parents here and a rumoured eighteen grade one spots). The principal, Mrs. Kruk, an ancient anorexic in a grey striped suit, arrives at seven, bringing morning coffee, yet more doughnuts and the coveted application forms.

"Good morning, parents, and thank you for your patience." Mrs. Kruk smiles the smile of the school administrator who can give parents what they want. "Thank you for your patience and dedication to your children and our school." She does a quick, silent head count and announces, "They're all in. Take a form and fill it out and then go home. All your kids are in."

Block Party

Every year we have this block party. It's close off the street, meet your neighbour, pass the potato salad and God Bless America. For one evening, we all get together and have a really good time. You have to go if you're any kind of neighbour at all, but we do have a pretty good time, at least I do. Some years we sit out on our lawn chairs in the middle of the street until eleven o'clock, even if it is a weeknight. The kids bring out their skateboards and roller blades and race around on the street all drunk on Pepsi and the freedom of being allowed to rule the pavement without fear of being mowed down by cars. The grown-ups find out stuff about each other. Like Arty Parks had chemo but he's all done now. And Janey Matthew's granddaughter, Ange, made it into law school, which almost makes up for Ange's little sister, Caroline, getting herself knocked up when she was barely a freshman. And the Spences are sending their boys to Canisius, the Catholic high school. It's a long drive, but Alfie, the older boy, should have his licence by Christmas. And Mrs. Welsch's mother died right after they finally put her in that home. Like Arthur's still out of work, but he has a lead on something great. And just how bad Anita's arthritis is. And how Anthony's planning to run for office again. Dog Catcher. City Clerk. Property Inspector. If you can run for it, Anthony has. That guy sure must love to lose. And then there's the home renos. The Rays redid their whole living room. The Menzies their kitchen. The Martins are taking whoever's willing on a tour of their new deck.

After we clean up and go home, dragging our barbecues and our half-asleep grandkids and our fat asses into the privacy of our own castles, it's all over for another year. Back at home, we peer out from our windows and porches and front stoops and watch each other's comings and goings. The Parkses next door in the big white house never trim their hedge. We call it *Afro hedge*. All Ricky (that's the wife) does outside is yell at her dogs. She's got at least eight golden retriever puppies at a time and the yard is like a circus camp for dogs. There are striped plastic hoops for the dogs to jump through, little balance beams, some weird triangle things, what looks like a slide, and all kinds of other stuff. Lots of different shaped thingies—geometrical shapes, mostly all different colours of the rainbow. It looks like some fucked-up French art exhibit or something. *Fucked-up lawn art*, we call it. The Parkses have a pool, but since their kids left home (two to college, one to the marines and one to jail), the pool is for the puppies now—their reward for whatever sick-ass stuff Ricky makes them do with all that yard geometry.

When it's not block party day, starting about five o'clock, I sit on the front porch, sipping my gin and tonic and waiting for the paperboy. I listen to Ricky yelling at her dogs. She doesn't just yell; she makes noises like a gorilla giving birth. I sit on the porch with my drink and think about ways to get back at her for ruining the neighbourhood. At least once a week I get out Gus's old John Deere and do the lawn, just to drown her out. I ride by and salute her, but she knows what I'm up to. At least I hope she does.

Also from the porch I can see the Spences across the street. Appee Spence is always in his driveway, working on some car. He's got one of those back trolleys he lies out on and most of the time all I can see of him is half his paunch and his spindly little legs sticking out from the underside of some Buick that'll never move again. He loves cars in a way that makes you admire him, even if he does hate human beings in a way that makes you shiver. Every street has one of those guys on it, I guess. Some have two or three, but ours is a pretty good street overall.

I didn't always live on this street. Some did. Addie—that's the love of my life—she has. She's not legally my wife, but we're as good as married and we've been together almost ten years now. It's Addie's house, all in her name, but I have my Caddy on its blocks in my side of the garage and my workshop in the basement and my dining room chair for doing crosswords and my living room chair for watching football and tennis and CNN. I tell her we're spending our golden years together and we are. Addie says, "Shush, Honey. Gold, platinum or silver. Let's just enjoy our time while we're here." And she's right and we do.

Addie was born here in this house when it was her father's. Right upstairs in our bedroom. Right on that horsehair mattress her mother had hauled in from the farm. Those who were not just born here, but whose folks lived here even before they were born, have a kind of special status on the street. There's four or five generations of Tregasers and Parkses and Spenses lived on this block. My gal, Addie, she'd be second generation Tregaser if she kept her name, and then her son Andy lives in the Millers' house on the corner. So his kids make four generations. It's not the Millers' house any more—hasn't been for twenty-five years, but we call it the Miller house. I never even knew any Millers.

Before I moved in with Addie, I hit some hard times. My wife Emma, my first wife, she was a looker but she wasn't so pretty after five or six drinks. That meant, most nights after eight or nine o'clock, she was looking pretty ugly. Her cheeks would get real red and her eyes all full of fire and she'd go after me. She threw our wedding dishes at me. She threw the fireplace tongs at me. She threw potted plants and ashtrays and bottles of hairspray at me. She threw everything at me but her beer glass. She only drank beer from a glass, never a bottle. That was as close as she had to a golden rule: thou shalt not throw thy beloved beer at thy lawfully wedded husband. Sometimes she hit me with whatever she winged at me and sometimes she missed. Once she threw a begonia plant right through the kitchen window. I'd say, "Holy Mother of Christ, don't I make good money? Don't I let you live the life, the good life, while I bust my balls to pay for it?" She'd throw more stuff. Then she would cry and caterwaul and carry on. The kids would hide in their beds and I'd just walk. I was outta there. I could take her trying to kill me but I couldn't take her wanting me to make her all better. I'd just walk out the door and keep on walking. She was breaking my heart but it felt good to be the one to walk. Sometimes I only walked as far as my 1965 Caddy convertible on blocks in the back yard. I'd climb in and light a smoke and sit out there watching the stars. It was like being right out in nature, at the lake or in the mountains out there in that car.

Other times I'd walk down the road to my brother Pete's place and the two of us would go into town for a beer. When I'd come knocking on his door, Pete was always glad to see me. "Hey, little brother," he'd say, even though I'm six two and weighed at least 190, even in those days. "Hey, little brother, you look like you need cheering up. Let's go into town and smell the pussy cats." Then he'd wink at me like we were off to do something really dastardly. But we'd just go to the Arm and Hammer, the little neighbourhood bar, and have a few. The worst we ever did was lean in a little up against the waitress when she was standing close to take our order or give us our drinks. I never cheated on Emma. I was a good husband. Better than she deserved.

One night I came home from a night out with Pete and Emma was in the sack with some scrawny, naked low-life. It was late and I came into the room quiet so as not to wake Emma. There he was. Right there in my bed, right next to my wife. I almost didn't see him. I almost climbed into my bed next to my wife right on top of him. My eyes adjusted to the light and Low-Life and I just stared at each other. Emma was passed out next to him. Not asleep but passed out. After eighteen years of marriage I knew the difference. The kids, thank God, were asleep, except for Jimmy, who was sixteen and out raising hell with his own kind.

Low-Life looked sad with his wrinkly eyelids and thin lips that struggled to stretch around his teeth. He said nothing but it was like he was trying to say, "Hey. You and I, bud. We gotta survive in this world and that means we gotta do some things we're not proud of. A woman like Emma, a beautiful woman, you couldn't blame me for getting tangled up with a woman like that, could you?" I turned and fled my own bedroom, my own wife and my own house, and went out and tried to sleep in the Caddy. I didn't sleep much. Instead of sleeping, I thought about doing some pretty awful stuff to Emma and the low-life, but even that long night, when any bastard would wallow and maybe lash out and no one would blame him, I knew I wouldn't hurt them. I thought about what a gutless coward I was and how Emma was right not to be able to stand me. I couldn't stand me, either. I thought about hanging myself in the basement and how Emma would find me dangling there all blue-lipped and done, done, done, when she came down to switch a load of laundry, and how she'd probably just carry right on, back up the stairs, cursing that the washing machine was old and sometimes left streaks of soap on the clothes, but then I thought, what if one of the kids found me instead of Emma? Where would be the satisfaction in that?

All this explains how I ended up at Pete's cabin out on Eighteen Mile Creek with no electricity and the only running water running right past the cabin door in the form of the creek. It was okay, though, but lonely. I had the Caddy towed out there even though it cost a hundred bucks to tow it that far—thirty miles. This was after I came home from work one day and found out Emma had changed the locks on me, which was about the time Emma had Low-Life installed permanently on my side of the bed. She said some things to me that I won't repeat. Pete's wife, Ellie, said I should be nice and civilized for the sake of the kids and all. I meant to but the most nice and civilized I could be was to just stay away. One time, a few weeks after the shit blew, I went to one of Allison's Little

League games. Allison was twelve and hated Little League. She thought it wasn't ladylike. She wanted to be in her room, putting on makeup and doing her nails, but I had put my foot down. She was a good pitcher since third grade and I wasn't about to let her give it all up for her new love of seventh grade boys. Anyway, she was there on the mound in her Hammee's Hardware uniform pitching with that bored, cool—my stupid parents are making me stand here—look on her face. That face, which months before had never been smeared with anything more sinister than jam or dirt, now was covered with globs of makeup—rouge, lipstick, mascara and purple eye shadow. She looked like a Little League hussy, truth be told. The truth is what I told her at the inning break.

"Dad?" she said, not looking at me and her voice trembling like it had been me who'd changed the locks. Like I was the one who asked to break up her family.

"Honey," I said. "You look like a little hussy with all that junk on your face. I'll walk you to the clubhouse and you can go in there and wash it off."

She was never one to take criticism. Any little comment— tie your shoes; sit up at the table; no, you may not be excused—and she'd be crying. She wasn't the youngest but she was the baby of the family. Right there in the field she started crying and hissing at me that I was messing up her makeup and that she hated softball and was going to quit if I didn't leave her alone and how come I never said anything and then when I did, why couldn't I just shut up?

"There, there, Baby," I said, because that's what I always called her.

Then her voice sounded tinny like her mother's and she said, "Just fuck off, Dad. I'm not a baby. I'm a hussy. Remember?"

Then I smacked her like parents do when their kids are

really lippy and need to get in line. Not really hard or any-thing. I just smacked her real soft. It felt—I can't describe it—terrifying but electric to have her warm cheek in contact with my hand. It had been two weeks since I'd seen any of them. I'd been at the cabin alone or at work. I hadn't touched anyone in two weeks, and here I was slapping my little girl in front of all the kids and all their smug, judgmental, not separated parents.

And then the umpire was there, and he said, Mr. Cowie, I'm going to have to ask you to leave the field. The game is starting. So I backed up off the field watching my baby, Allison, with her hand on her cheek and her eyes blinking hard to keep the tears from making the black rims around her eyes look any worse. She wouldn't look at me, but the next inning she pitched was a no-hitter. That never happens in softball. Especially never in twelve-year-old girls' softball. That girl was a Tasmanian devil on the pitcher's mound. I was proud of her but then I saw her mother and the low-life in the stands. There they were, out flaunting it in public, holding hands and sitting close like they were pretty darned pleased with them-selves. After the game Allison and one of the other girls went over to them. The other girl, Marie, must have been Low-Life's daughter. I'm sure she was and the four of them climbed into the low-life's sedan and drove off.

I lived in the cabin by the creek for four years while Emma and Low-Life sicced his lawyer brother on me. They took me to town, got everything except the Caddy. And then, get this, I had to pay *her* money for cheating on me and divorcing me. I made an okay salary at the plant at the time so I could manage things, especially living at the cabin. Ellie and Pete said I should have had my own lawyer to fight hers but I wouldn't do it. The divorce took two years longer than she wanted because I wouldn't help her out with it. As it turned out, she didn't need my help. She did pretty good and if she had had a head for money, which she never did, she would have been pretty well off.

As it turned out, she and Low-Life partied it all away and ended up losing the house. That was later, though, and by that time I'd already moved on. That was around the time she came down with the kidney thing and had to go on dialysis. I felt bad for her but not that bad. It wasn't like she got what she deserved or anything, like what went around came around, but at least she got something. Anyway, it was the booze that killed her in the end. The end was closer than any of us thought, just the year after I moved out of the cabin and here on Rosedale Street with Addie.

Before Addie knew me, she had this charmed life. Well, not her childhood. She spent that picking string beans and strawberries on her dad's farm every summer. She went to grade one when she was four years old because her older sisters all went to school, so she begged her mom to let her go. Her mom finally said okay. After the first day of sitting up straight and keeping quiet in the one-room schoolhouse, she walked the two miles home with her sisters and cried and begged not to have to go to school ever again. Her mom said, *no dice*. Her mom said, *you made your bed*. Her mom was tough as nails and Addie thanks her for it to this day. I do too because she passed some of that steel will on to Addie.

They were a hard-working family though her dad did run off to California a few times. Her mom said he just had wanderlust. He never wanted to be a farmer. When he was seventeen he'd moved into town and apprenticed himself to a plumber. His dad came into town after him, said he was underage, which he was, and brought him home to the farm. So maybe the childhood wasn't happy because her dad never spoke and ran off now and then and her parents had their own bedrooms and Addie always knew she was a mistake, born six years after the older three girls, or maybe her dad wanted to try one more time for a boy, she wasn't sure, and it was a lonely childhood being so much younger than the other girls and out on the farm and with her parents too old and too tired to do much for her. But Addie says too much happiness in childhood only makes you miserable later on. Makes you not prepared.

Anyway, then came the charmed part. She met Angus at an art class. He was a reporter then, and she was learning to sculpt. He enlisted and they went off to Virginia for the war. She worked in a lab there for the army and he was an officer. When the war was over they moved back to Aurora and into this house with her mother. It was supposed to be temporary. She always wanted her own house and a white leather sofa and a bigger dining room and a second bathroom, but they stayed here and raised their kids. And it was a charmed life. They went out dancing on Friday and Saturday nights. In the summers, they hung out at the club, Willow Bend. It wasn't one of those high and mighty doctors' and lawyers' clubs, just a regular family-type swim and tennis club. They had picnics and the kids swam and put on plays and ran through the woods and the grown-ups drank martinis and played tennis and drank martinis and gossiped and drank martinis and shared hors d'oeuvres and drank martinis and danced and drank martinis and flirted and joked and then did it all over again.

It was all good until one day Gus keeled over at his desk in the attic. He didn't die right away but he wouldn't go to the doctor. He said it was a cold. Dr. Hilderman came over, his wife was a friend of Addie's, played bridge with her for twenty-five years, and told Gus he was having a heart attack and should get to the hospital. But Gus said no, it was a cold and he had work to do. He rode his bike into the village to get to the post office and drop off his stories (he ran a freelance writing business out of the attic) and rode it home again. Then he climbed into his bed and dropped dead.

Addie didn't take it well. She froze up. Her friends brought her casseroles and self-help books. Her sons made tasteless jokes about their dad's still horny, rotting carcass. She thanked her friends but couldn't eat the casseroles and wouldn't read the self-help books. "A lot they know," she said. She was outraged that the books and some friends tried to say they knew how she felt, knew what she was going through. She laughed at her sons' jokes but the inside of her mouth tasted like cardboard and she lost about twenty pounds in three months. She wasn't big to begin with. Her sons told her she had killed him with her blueberry pies. They thought that was uproariously funny. She laughed with them but never made another blueberry pie. She started to volunteer in the slums of Buffalo, bringing food and baby clothes to mentally challenged teenage mothers. She said it was the only thing she did that made her feel better. This was when she started to develop her view that it was better not to be born. "I'm not saying I don't love my life," she'd say. "Honey, I'm not saying that. I'm just saying that if I'd been given a say in it, I might just as well have said *no thanks*."

Once, six months after Gus died, Addie's old friend from high school, Margie Witherspoon, who was also a widow, invited Addie to a girls' night out. Addie went because she thought she should. The women all brought fancy snacks— cream cheese apricot balls and pasty puffs and aspic salads— and they sat around together twittering and cackling. Margie was warm and welcoming and said to Addie about eighty times, "It's so good you came, dear. I told you we just have the best time." After Margie said that she laughed heartily and the other women joined in.

The women talked about their kids and their grandchildren and their trips to Florida, their gardens, their hysterectomies and their flat arches. Whenever there was the a pause in conversation, they filled it with their at first meaningless but finally aggressive laughter. They talked about which grocery store was the best in town, Tops Market or Grocerytown. Tops had the better deal on cereal (ha, ha, ha). The produce was fresher at Grocerytown (chuckle, chuckle).

Addie knew she was depressed after Gus died. At the widows' shindig her sadness turned into rage. She hated Margie and her nice old-lady girliness. She begrudged these women their hollow smiles, their meaningless patter and most of all their addiction to laughing. The less funny, the more laughter, that was their law. Secretly she wished them ill at their dental appointments and blood tests and eye exams. She hoped their grandchildren would move away or drop out of school or become unwed mothers or all of the above. She loathed their perms, their pantsuits, their loafers and the colour of their lipstick, though she had known Margie and some of these other women most of her life and never had any bad feelings towards them. She was grateful for the fury that swept over her when she was smiling and nodding at these women and thankful that it stayed with her well into the long, sleepless night that followed. Since Gus died, she hadn't been sleeping at all, really. Daytime was for faking it and getting through, nighttime was for obsessions, recriminations and wading through pain. Anything that could pull her out of that cycle, even petty, unjustifiable rage, was an improvement.

It was years later that she understood that it wasn't the women or their taste in clothes or food or their dullness or even their insane cheerfulness that bothered her so. It was the widows' club that they wanted her to join. In high school, Margie had been in every club—sewing, student newspaper, Girl Scouts. She had never wanted Addie to join then, but now, now that they were no longer young but not quite old and their lives were basically ruined by the weak hearts of their husbands, now she was welcoming her with open arms. The motto of the club might have been, "Laugh in the face of your pointless existence."

Two days after Addie had her girls' night out, Addie and I met. Bill and Annie Tregaser were going to a cocktail party and dance at Dock O' the Bay out by the waterfront and they brought Addie along. I knew Bill from before; we'd worked together years back when they were building the second bridge. All the young fellows worked on that bridge. I was there because Bill had called me up and told me they were coming and that he was bringing Addie. I told him I'd had enough with women but he said that Addie was a prize and if I let her get away without at least saying hello to her, I deserved to drink myself to death alone out in the cabin. "This is your chance," he told me. "And if we get there in time for happy hour the drinks are half-price and there's free chicken wings."

So I was there, feeling a little warm and rosy from the food and drinks and with grease from the wings on my fingers. There was Addie, thinner than Emma, with small dark eyes and a helmet of thick grey hair, but a fine-looking woman. Bill introduced us and Addie told a joke about two geezers on a date. "There were these two old geezers on a date. They were both dressed in their best clothes, but the lady geezer had an umbrella with her, which she held over her head at all times.

The guy geezer said to the lady geezer, 'why do you carry that parasol, me lady?'" At this point Addie faltered. "Damn," she said. "It was something about not melting like the wicked witch. I'm sorry, Joe. I couldn't tell a joke to save my life." And here she sounded almost testy. "If you knew me at all, you'd know that about me."

"I know it now," I said. It was maybe the only tactful, sensitive thing I ever said to anyone and probably just a fluke but it was like putting a key in a lock and opening up a door.

"Yes," she said, "you do," and her eyes filled up. "But I'm not sad," she said. "Or at least I'm less sad than I've been." Then she apologized for crying in front of me.

"It's okay," I said, and even though Emma's tears were the one thing I could never bear, I felt good sitting there with Addie pouring on the waterworks next to me. I felt honoured; like I was a friend of hers. Then she said her eyes were tan BBS; how she had always wanted big blue eyes like mine instead of her measly bird-peck eyes.

I said I thought she had superb eyes, not tan, a nice light brown. She told me to *watch it*; she wasn't one to take compliments, she said. She was just raised that way.

A few weeks after that night, I started staying over at Addie's house on Rosedale Street. She had a room in the basement that one of her sons had fixed up for him and his girlfriend when he was finishing high school and wanted privacy. The room was called *the coal bin* though it wasn't a bad room—less damp than the cabin, and cleaner for sure. When Addie's kids were around I slept down in the coal bin or at least made a show of going off down there at first. After, I'd make my way upstairs to Addie's room. Her kids were grown up then and out of the house mostly. They had girlfriends of their own they'd brought home so it was silly to put on a show like that, but it was what Addie wanted and what Addie wanted, I wanted to give her.

This year is the tenth Rosedale Street block party I've been at, I say to Addie as we sit on our porch (her porch, but really our porch now) in the early afternoon and watch the preparations. My daughter, Allison, is coming this year. She'll bring her two girls, and Addie's son, who lives around the corner, will be here with his mob. The Spences already have their chairs and table and barbecue on the curb. The barricades don't go up until four o'clock, but some kids are skateboarding on the street, getting ready to claim it.

"Let me get us a refill," I say to Addie. I'm interrupting her. She's been talking about the election. How the Republicans are all crooks. She's wearing me down on that one, even if I've been a Republican all my life. It's personal with her and if she wants me to vote Democrat, I will—they're all crooks, whatever party, but she's heard me say that often enough. She doesn't mind being interrupted. It's not like I haven't heard her on this merry-go-round before. She smiles at me and hands me her glass and says, "Just a few more drops, Honey." She calls everyone "Honey," but when she says that to me, I still get a thrill. I get up off the wooden chair I built and stained myself (all the porch furniture I made for her) and head toward the kitchen. The porch screen door I painted yellow for Addie (to match the yellow daisies in the window pots I made for the porch railing) swings shut after me. The door doesn't slam but it shuts solid and makes a good sturdy, satisfying sound. I like to build things to last and Addie likes that about me. In the kitchen, I've added some shelves for her summer dishes and hooks on the wall for her coffee cups. I built special holders for the blades of her Cuisinart under the upper cabinet next to the sink. I've done a lot around here, even if it'll never be my house.

I fix the drinks and take them through the dining room. I stop there for a minute to scan the pictures on the walls. There are her sons and their kids, her mom and dad, Gus as a little boy and Gus and she smiling together at some beach. There is a colour picture of me and even two little ones of Allison's kids, but I know they're just token. It's kind of Addie to put them on the wall, but they look temporary next to the serious black and white family photos. If you took down one of the old pictures, there would be a yellow rectangle or reproach on the spot on the wall. Not so with my picture or Allison's little tykes. I look hard at the picture of Gus with his greased-back grey hair, his manly face with large, womanish lips. It's understood around here that he was a better man than me. He was witty and dapper and if I hear one more time what a great dancer he was, I might do something I'd regret. He made a lot of money and never for one second doubted himself. Not for one second.

The big black and white picture of Gus and the shabby colour snapshot of me next to it shows it's no contest. Even I know that she chose me precisely for that reason—because there would never be any question of her feelings for me competing with her memories of Gus. I was a safe choice because I would never eclipse him. I walk through the living room with my chair in it, the padded, white rocker with the extra cushion. Just like Archie Bunker, I've got a chair for watching tennis and football and the news and even her kids ,who think I'm dumber than my granddaughter's pet turtle, don't sit in my chair, at least not when I'm around. I walk past my chair, knowing that it must have been Gus's chair before it was mine, but it doesn't bother me. It's mine now.

I take our drinks out to the porch and hand Addie hers.

"Cheers," she says.

"Cheers," I say back, and sit down next to the love of my life. Together we wait for the party to start.

She was Kate

In the dream everyone is right there by her bed. The director, the cameraman and the other actors all standing around. Kate feels like the little girl in *The Exorcist*. At any moment the bed will start shaking and she will be forced to make all sorts of inhuman, retching sounds. Someone should make *The Exorcist* from the little girl's perspective. She once read a book where they did that with Grendel, the monster in *Beowulf*, and another one about King Arthur's court from the perspective of the women.

"Be Katharine Hepburn in *Suddenly Last Summer*," the director says. He has a confident, encouraging expression. She can't believe this. If he had said Elizabeth Taylor, it might have been credible. She has short dark hair and she knows how to smoke a cigarette, but there is no way she can be Katharine Hepburn.

She tries, though. "My niece lacerates herself with memory.

That is her illness." It is the only line from the movie she can remember and she isn't even sure she has it right. She feels like Katharine Hepburn, though. Skinny and totally in control.

"Good. Now be Judy Garland. When she was the little girl, of course."

To stall, she says, "Kansas or Oz?"

"It's your dream," the director says, throwing the responsibility right back at her. Then an amazing thing happens. She understands that it is her dream and this is one audition she isn't going to blow. She looks down at the little ruby red slippers on her feet (even her feet are little) and then the clock radio starts to blast the sports.

The best part is remembering without opening her eyes or moving that she had the dream, that she was Katharine Hepburn and almost Judy Garland. She wants to live in black and white or forties Technicolor for the rest of the day. There is no reason to go to work.

It takes forty-five minutes to find her keys. They are in the pocket of the jeans she wore last night and kicked under the bed with all the other dirty clothes. She has been skipping breakfast lately because there is only stale bread and cereal and the milk is older than the best before date. It was probably still all right yesterday. Certainly the day before. She should have used it up then. There is no way she is going to risk it now. Anyway, avoiding breakfast gives her an edge all morning at work.

Before she leaves, Kate hugs Camus, the dog she inherited from Andy, and gives him some water and then lets him out by the back stairs. Camus is a gangly, oversized mutt with raw patches checkering his haunches where there should be coarse, matted, golden fur. He is used to spending the day roaming the back lanes, scavenging and picking fights with other dogs. The apartment is too small for him, but she couldn't stand to give him away.

When Kate met Andy, only a year ago, but forever for a nineteen-year-old girl, she was in the coffee shop at the Aberdeen Hotel, skipping grade twelve French class and reading Rainer Maria Rilke. It made Kate feel smart to read Rilke and it made her happy to skip French. The bar was attached to the coffee shop and she noticed Andy when they were kicking him out of it. Andy was shouting, "He's my seeing-eye dog. You can't throw us out. That's illegal. I know some important people. I'm important. Camus is important. You can't do this." Andy's eyes were blazing—there was nothing blind about them. Camus just sat there, grinning and panting, not taking sides.

The bouncer didn't talk. He just pushed Andy closer to the door, prodding him with the flat of his hand. Andy's face was beaming with righteous indignation; not the alcohol-induced kind, but the serious, naïve kind. The scruffy pup was barking short, hard yelps because Andy was squeezing him against the inside of his jacket, trying to shield him from the bouncer.

Kate stayed in the coffee shop, not reading, but thinking about Andy's nerve. She thought, What for? What a troublemaker, but she liked him. She liked that he wore striped purple pants and that his outrageousness was totally out of his hands; he had no idea.

On the way out of the hotel coffee shop, Kate tripped over the dog and then the step. She landed on the gravel, mouth first somehow. Andy laughed a huge yuk-yuk kind of laugh, a laugh so unself-conscious it rang out on the downtown street like an obscenity. He stopped dead when he saw the blood dripping down her chin and said, "My God. You're going to die. He's a seeing-eye dog. I'm training him. He didn't mean it." The dog just stayed put as if it was no big deal. Kate sat on the gravel lot, tasting blood. Andy kneeled down beside her, trying to coax the dog to lick the blood off Kate's chin. "Come on, Camus. Come on, Cam. Kiss it better. Camus, Camus, Camus," but the dog refused to get involved.

Kate had never cut herself badly before. As it turned out, this cut was not serious, but it seemed like it at first. She had a child's fascination with her own blood. It was exotic like a crime or a revelation running down her mouth, her throat, and staining her t-shirt. Her lip was pulsating. "Spurting," she said. "It's spurting like a fountain."

"Come on, Camus, you schmuck, apologize," Andy said. He jumped up and whooped just in case he hadn't already drawn enough attention to himself. People on the street stared at them. "Come on, I'll take you to the hospital. The Misery's just a fifteen-minute walk." He meant the Misericordia hospital.

"It's all right. I think the bleeding is going to stop." Kate touched her lip tentatively and found a crust forming. She tried to hide her disappointment that her unexpected outburst of blood could so abruptly come to an end. Nothing serious would happen. Then Andy said he would like to kiss her entire body, everywhere except her lip (where it would hurt) as a penance for him and Camus. Kate wasn't shocked or very surprised. It seemed like since she saw Andy, the two of them had been ad-libbing a love ritual, something long forgotten, but they found it perfectly intact. Everything that happened was appropriate.

Soon they were lovers and her first apartment became their apartment, but he kept the ritual of never kissing her on the mouth. She'd tried to talk him out of it or force him into it. She said, "Look, there's barely even a scar," but he told her he'd done enough damage. That refusal to kiss her face-to-face had infuriated her long after Andy left. When Andy lit out, Kate inherited Camus. After a while, she had thrown out Andy's toothbrush and razor and given away his winter jacket and workboots. She had torn pages out of his copy of *Rules for Radicals* to try to use for rolling paper and thrown away what was left of the book, but she had kept the dog.

On the way downstairs she drops yesterday's paper through the mail slot of Marianella's door. Marianella is a massage therapist. She lives in the apartment below Kate's with her son, Luke. Luke was born blind. He is three years old and wakes up in the middle of the night smashing his little body against the walls and shrieking. Kate hears him sometimes at night, but during the day he is always sweet, running over to touch Kate's face and ask her to read to him. Marianella wants the newspaper so she can do papier mâché with Luke. He likes the cold glue oozing through his fingers and would put it all over himself if his mother would let him.

Kate works at Athlete's World in the postal shipping department. The company ships sports equipment and clothing to schools all over Canada and even to Germany, where there is a Canadian air force base. She likes the names of the faraway places: Ucluelet, St. Teresa Point, Inuvik, and Lahr, Germany. She likes that from Inuvik to Vancouver Island, schoolchildren use the same soft leather tetherballs and the same number five Louisville Slugger baseball bats.

The best part of Kate's workday is from eight-thirty until nine. She has the third floor to herself. She keeps the radio off and looks over the orders waiting to be packed, stamped, addressed and sent downstairs. That is her whole job except for sweeping up at the end of the day. Today, like most days, it seems like there are an impossible number of orders for one day. Before nine she can drink coffee at her worktable without getting caught. She wonders how this small act of defiance can give such pleasure. It is because she is too disengaged to think except in short sputters. It is a good thing boredom, by itself, isn't powerful enough to start someone ripping up base-ball jerseys or smashing the postage meter with a floor hockey stick.

The pickers come at five after nine. She has already done three orders of six boxes—probably a record.

She has lunch with Mindy, who types invoices downstairs in the office. According to Mindy, the important thing about working in an office is being pleasant. Kate is glad she works in the shipping department. Mindy must not think Kate is very pleasant, but feels sorry for her because she has such awful taste in clothes and isn't engaged and will probably be stuck at Athlete's World forever; at least until the computers take over. Kate feels sorry for Mindy because she is getting married soon and because this wedding, really the idea of this wedding, is the most thrilling thing that has ever happened to Mindy. As far as Kate is concerned, Mindy is a polyester. She wants everything Kate would never want. Kate likes talking to Mindy because it reminds her that she really does have some things going for her. Kate wonders if Mindy feels the same way about Kate.

They are both nineteen, the youngest employees at Ath-lete's World. They are both still young enough to expect that something really wonderful will happen to them today or tomorrow that will alter everything. Being young is being small. They are so small that in all that bigness out there, there must be something, a word, a man, an accident, that was made to rescue them from a numb, Athlete's World life. The difference between them, Kate sees, is that Mindy has found her something. He is Gary Staminow, a halfback for the Blue Bombers, and he is going to marry her in the spring. Kate is still waiting for whatever it is to fall on her head, like one of those sixteen-ton cubes that get the really bad talent acts on *Talent America*. It isn't going to be a halfback.

"Did you say yes right away?" she asks. They have already eaten and made fun of Mr. Cranton, Mindy's high-blood-pressure boss, who wears pinstriped suits with his Reeboks running shoes. *Dress for success*, he always says (*suck-cess*, Kate tells Mindy).

"I wanted to, but I made him wait overnight," Mindy says. "I told him I wanted to talk to my parents first."

"Are you serious? What would you have done if they didn't want you to?" Kate knows the answer. Mindy told her about the magazine article, "What to Do When He Proposes," a month ago.

"How could they not like him? Anyway, I never asked them. I just wanted Gary to sweat a bit first. It's kind of like a superstition for good luck. I read this article about it."

"Oh yeah." Kate has a habit of saying *oh yeah* at work. She says it so much that she's starting to use it at home with her friends. There is a secret about it, though. It doesn't mean *oh yeah* as in agreement, but *oh yeah* as in *why don't you drop dead*, as in *please shut up before I tell you how much I could care less*.

"Oh yeah, I got a postcard from Andy. He's in Vancouver and Cindy's pregnant and he's totally happy. They're going to eat the placenta."

"That is sick," Mindy says, looking overly disgusted. Her eyes go mushy and she makes a face. "Isn't that illegal? It's so gross." Mindy likes hearing about Andy because he is so appalling. He is like her grandfather's war stories: part of another world, an imaginary crazy world filled with grotesquery and surprises.

Kate is a little proud of having spent almost a year with Andy—a circus freak by Athlete's World norms—and a little embarrassed too. She wants to say to Mindy that he really will eat the thing. It will be some kind of spiritual experience for him. Just like when he blew up their television, and when he gave all his clothes to the Sally Ann except for one pair of green workpants, a Clash t-shirt, his jacket and workboots and a sweater an old girlfriend had made for him. Just like the mushroom obsession or the spray paint frenzy. For Mindy, the point is that he is outrageous, not transcendental. Kate doesn't feel like explaining. Besides, when she was with Andy, she wasn't so impressed with his spirituality. "You're a junkie," she told him. "A mushroom junkie, a spray paint junkie, a sex junkie, a spir-it-u-ality junkie. So what."

He had picked up his electric guitar and, without plugging it in, started playing that Neil Young anthem for all lost boys, "The Needle and the Damage Done." He had been totally absorbed. For all he knew, he was Neil Young.

"A Neil Young junkie," she had shouted before she could stop herself.

He stopped playing and started to laugh—his favourite way of not explaining himself—but then he just went quiet.

After lunch Kate is glad to be back on the shipping floor, alone except for the order pickers, who keep their distance, maybe so they can slack off unobserved and maybe because Kate is an anomaly to them. She is the only woman on the floor and the first woman who has ever worked in the shipping department at Athlete's World. Some people she sees outside work think it's cool that she's a shipper, but she makes the pickers nervous. They are extra sweet and flirtatious with the younger women in the office, like Mindy, and they are crude and buddy-buddy with each other. They are uncomfortable flirting with Mindy in front of Kate and uncomfortable acting like the boys around her too. Today she is glad she doesn't have to talk to them except for *hi* and *see ya later* and *oh yeah*. At 4:25 she sweeps the floor and puts everything away.

Kate walks home in a state of numb summer ecstasy. I'm a freedom junkie, she thinks. Freedom of movement. Freedom from Athlete's Foot World. Freedom to not have any have-tos. Four-thirty makes her delirious. She would like to keep on walking to the city limits, past the perimeter highway, into some farmer's wheat field at dusk. She would like to walk right out of this life. Halfway home, when she's on the meridian, trying to cross Portage Avenue, the delirium goes sour. On the other side she stops to buy some celery soup and crackers at the 7-11, and thinks she'll just go home and eat and go to sleep. It occurs to her that she could be, like everyone else, leading a life of quiet desperation, but she is Kate, not everyone else, so she decides to go home, have soup, and read a book in the bathtub.

At home Camus is waiting on the fire escape for her, hysterically glad to see her. Marianella's door is open and Kate calls hello. Luke is listening to television and tracing the lines on the couch with his fingers. Marianella's apartment always smells good, like incense and fresh baking. "Come down for tea later, if you feel like it," Marianella says.

"Sure," Kate says.

Upstairs, she feeds Camus and makes her soup; comfort food. She eats a half a box of crackers while the soup is heating up. Three months ago, she could have quit work, gone to Vancouver, and talked Andy back into loving her. Right now, she could call Mindy and ask her to go to a bar. Mindy is always saying they should do that. Or she could go downstairs and drink herbal tea and talk about Luke and harmonic convergences. Neither of these is an enticing option. She is Kate. She is nineteen and tedium is festering like a stubborn coldsore that doesn't go away because she keeps irritating it with her tongue. Even her boredom feels weak and recycled. She decides that tomorrow she will plan her escape from Athlete's World. She will travel in Europe, go to university and fall in love. She will make all those connections. Starting tomorrow. After supper, she reads in the bath until the water is tepid. She calls down to Marianella that she is too tired tonight for tea, but thanks anyway.

In the dream, Luke is in her apartment. Camus is comatose on the kitchen mat. He growls in his sleep, but doesn't wake up. Luke is applying papier mâché to her body. She moves to make it easier for him. The strips of paper are cool and slimy with glue. He is working on her back and her rib cage. He uses long strips and wraps them like bandages. It is uncomfortable to be touched by such a little child, vaguely sensual and vaguely not nice, but she reasons that he is blind and must touch. She is afraid of suffocating, but because he is blind she thinks he will not understand if she tells him to stop. She turns to look at him, willing him to stop. His white, empty eyes, the colour of milk and cream separating, stare back.

There is a terrifying smile on his face. The smile of someone who has never seen a smile. His fat hands hold a wide, dripping strip of newspaper. They reach out to cover her eyes. The glue is everywhere in the bed and the room and it smells like yeast. The dream has made everything in the room smaller except the little boy. He is lifesize. Kate screams but no sound comes out.

It is suddenly morning and there is light from the window and the sports on the radio. The Expos won. The Blue Bombers lost. The room quietly breathes daylight and regains its composure. Camus whines gingerly and puts his wet nose against her cheek, telling her to get up and feed him and go to work A few minutes later, Kate sits in the kitchen, watching the toaster so the toast doesn't burn. Camus, already fed, is out on his morning ramble.

Kate knows that right now, her life is nothing serious. She is in a gap, a space between the things about being alive that matter. There are things. She calls them the YESes. The first YES she remembers was falling in a swimming pool when she was three. Her eyes were wide. She wasn't afraid. She floated down like she was in amniotic fluid. Because of the chlorine, the water was aqua blue, a watery aqua blue, the correct colour for water. That's all she remembers except that somebody must have saved her. She remembers a large shape like the shadow of a whale coming towards her in the water. It must have been her father.

The second YES was a swamp behind the soccer field at school when she was nine. She had two friends at school, Sherry, who was blonde and giggled all the time, and Melinda, whom Kate liked only because Sherry did. Some days Sherry and Melinda liked each other so much that they didn't like Kate. On one of those days, Kate found the swamp. She was going to run away and never come back, but only about twenty feet into the woods behind the school was her swamp. Everything there was rotting or crumbling and smelled strong and sweet and heavy like fog. There were huge fallen trees covered with crusty green moss, a tiny creek that barely moved and toadstool mushrooms. Everything was in the process of becoming part of everything else. She could hear the children in the soccer field, but their voices sounded like static from a distant radio, poorly tuned in. The swamp was green and looked musty and wet, the way a swamp should and does. She could see and breathe, and she shrank like Alice until she was a very little girl, and she wasn't separate and she didn't care about Sherry and Melinda.

Meeting Andy that first time, tripping over Camus and falling on her face was another YES. At the time, she'd thought it was about Andy: YES to growing up and falling in love. Now, Andy wasn't important, but the thrill of free-falling when she tripped over the dog, the brashness of gravel imbedded in her skin and the taste of her own blood were what made that moment count. She'd held nothing back, embraced the world face-first and lived to tell about it.

Kate digs out some remnants of peanut butter from the jar and spreads it on her toast. She grabs her book in one hand and her toast in the other and heads off to work. Her mouth is full so she waves what's left of her toast at Marianella and Luke as she passes their open door on the way down the fire escape. Kate walks up Balmoral Street with the sun already high in the sky. The leaves on the elm trees are a shimmering green awning. The sky above them is an hallucinogenic prairie shade of blue. Around her, people are making their way to work or school, basking in the warm June day that is certain to be a scorcher. After a year, the tiny scar on her lip caused by her fall over Camus is almost completely invisible. Kate touches her tongue to the scar, and even through the remnants of peanut butter, it tastes like a sliver of solid silver.

Three Connected Stories:

Nathan at Large

Down the Rabbit Hole

Sierra

Nathan at Large

Dweebo-dweeb, square-headed Nathan grudged his way into the world one night in July while Lynette screamed, dug her nails into three shifts' worth of nurses and begged sweet baby Jesus for mercy. Dumb-headed Nathan plodded and poked his way out, the same way he did anything else. After twenty-six hours of this, the doctor announced that Mom was well over eleven centimetres dilated. "How can she be twelve centimetres?" a resident wanted to know. "We'll see," the doctor, who didn't believe in episiotomies, answered, as she readied the scalpel.

As Nathan began his lifelong task of worrying his parents with his peculiarities, his dad, Jack, paced the hallway reading old *New Yorkers*, appearing to have no idea where he was or why. He read a piece on Burt Lahr, the cowardly lion from *The Wizard of Oz*. He read how Lahr was never allowed to be anyone other than the cowardly lion, how he was depressed and angry and a bad father. He read a short story about shiny glass objects on a coffee table in the cottage of a woman who was trying to become a sea goddess. He read the goings on about town. No matter that they lived in Winnipeg, not New York. No matter that he had never been to New York and that the magazine was out of date by several years.

But then there was Nathan, blue-faced, red-bodied, big-mouthed, hair-challenged Nathan, screaming his newborn rage into his mother's exhausted, ecstatic face. Someone went to find Jack and introduce him to his son. "Look what the Lord brought us," Lynette crooned and Jack looked proud and happy and scared as if he'd just been cast in a great role he could only hope to fake his way through.

In the picture of the three of them together in the hospital, Lynette and Jack were smiling bleary-eyed like they'd been at an all-night session of church and Nathan's soon-to be-tan beady eyes were crammed shut. He was too tired from all the trouble he had already caused.

Lynette claimed she bonded with Nathan right away—the second she saw him. It was God's will, she always said, even when Nathan was old enough to argue with her. "What kind of God wills bonding for some babies and none for others?" he was asking by the time he was eight. "Was it God's will that I get a little sister like Gabbie, a one-person plague on my existence?" he wanted to know when he was nine and a half and Gabbie was seven. The answer to these questions was a version of *the Lord works in mysterious ways, trust the Lord, the Lord knows, count your blessings* or *for God's sake, leave your sister alone, for once.* By the time Nathan was eleven, he had stopped asking. It was no fun to keep winning an argument when your opponent was too irrational to ever concede.

Abigail, known to Nathan as Grabby Gabbie, flabby Gabbie, little crybaby crabby Gabbie, was two years younger than Nathan. She always would be. (Nyah nyah.) She was, in Nathan's view, skinny, weak, stupid and horrifically popular. She was voted the class president in grade four and Nathan knew the vote was not a response to her political savvy. She believed Baby Jesus was the prime minister. She inherited those ideas from Mom, but still. She did her little pom-pom routine instead of a speech and all those grade four suckers voted for her. Even some of the boys. It was beyond irresponsible, but there was nothing Nathan could do about it.

Lynette looked after everyone: the kids, Jack, the cat, the neighbour's cat, Gabbie's friends and, until they died, Jack's mother and her own parents. She managed by keeping a buzz going in her head almost all the time. The buzz whispered: The Lord is with me. The Lord is with me. Praise the Lord. The Lord is with me. It doesn't matter what my daddy did to my mommy when I was a little girl, cowering in the closet. It doesn't matter because the Lord is with me. It doesn't matter that I have a square-headed son whose only interests are torturing his sister and taking over the world. It doesn't matter that Jack loves books more than me or the kids. It doesn't matter that I have to do the nasty with Jack to get him to hold me and even then it's only for a little while before he extricates himself and snaps the condom off and reaches for his glasses and his book. It doesn't matter because the Lord is with me. It doesn't matter that I want, need, must have, it's God's will, a third child, and Jack is the only man on the planet who is obsessed with condoms no matter how apparently safe the time of the month is. Maybe he doesn't like to have his touch mine. But it doesn't matter because when I sing, the Lord is with me. It doesn't matter because when the Lord descends, I'll show Jack and everyone and they'll be on their knees beside me. And I'll be the Lord's bride. And there'll be no smelly rubber coming between us. Praise the Lord. I'm just a lowly wife and mother. I just want to serve Him. But the meek shall inherit. So I am meek, meek, meek. And Jack's going to be out in the cowshed when He descends. And he'll ask himself what he was doing reading *Harper's* in church, reading his big books all over town. Where will they get him? Not to the Kingdom of Heaven. I think not. Easier a camel than a rich man or a man obsessed with what's in his head. Jack isn't a rich man. He works in the library but not as a librarian. He's the security guard. Too smart to go to community college and learn how to work the library computers. Too smart to make enough money to support his loving family. He's not a rich man, but he does look like a camel when he hunches over me at night. He's only a hunchback when he's getting his earthly pleasure. Maybe one day, God will take pity on me and the condom will slip away and I'll get my next baby. Maybe one day, praise God.

The world hummed all around Jack. He liked the library where the hum was gentler. People sat in their carrels, caressing their books and thinking their own thoughts. No one hurried. No one shouted, *pay attention. Pay attention to me, goddammit.* Sometimes the spell was broken by a child throwing a fit in the front entrance. He didn't want to wear his mittens or some such. He wailed and ranted and his mother ended up hissing at him like an angry tabby, shoving the mitts on his flailing hands, and dragging him hard by the arm to the door.

At some point the child sensed the shame he was causing her, that he was desecrating this sacred place with his undisciplined wants. He crunched his body into a ball and went rigid and his mother carried him by his one uplifted arm quickly and brutally towards the checkout desk. When he finally stopped crying and then even whimpering, the sound of her furious whispering rose up. The words were not discernible, but there was deep rage flowing through them. People like that didn't belong in the library.

Jack made his rounds. No one was smoking in the bathrooms. Two teens kissed near the reserve section, but they were not groping or gyrating and it was easy not to see them. He found his way back to his secret spot: the ancient Japanese history section where there was almost never a patron and settled into reading the book he had hidden there. He was reading the complete works of Henry James. Jack was a completist. He liked to be thoroughly inside the voice and mind of one writer at a time. Hours, days and years pass this way. Often he stayed well past five o'clock and Lynette would have to call the library and have him paged. The voice on the PA would announce, "Jack Grunberg, please leave the library."

Gabbie had a Barbie and Skipper birthday. Only Gabbie and her best friend Jen were Barbies. All the other girls had to be Skippers. Jen and Gabbie went first at Pin-the-Barrette-on-the-Barbie-Face (Barf-face, Nathan called her). The Skippers had to wait. The Barbies took the first pieces of Marble Barbie cake with pink icing and roses. The cake had blonde hair, pink skin and blue party dress icing. Nathan was invited to the party, but he had to be Ken. Lynette said it was only fair. It was Gabbie's ninth birthday. Nathan wanted to be psycho-killer-atomic-bomb-man-Ken. It would be some party. But Gabbie got wind of his plan and told Lynette who told Jack who told Nathan to cut it out. "It's your sister's birthday," he said sternly. With fatherly authority. With too much severity.

Nathan knew Dad was overacting. He was overdoing the grown-up thing because he didn't want to be found out. He didn't want Nathan to know that he was a kid himself; a kid zipped up so tight inside a stuffy grown-up costume that he couldn't see out of the eyeholes and could hardly breathe. Like Nathan felt last Hallowe'en when he wore that rubber Tricky Dicky mask and carried a tape recorder that repeated, "My fellow Americans, cash is better than candy" on an infinite loop. Nathan felt sorry for Dad, which must have been what he wanted, because it made Nathan want to behave himself. Nathan would have tried to behave himself. He would have tried, but there were Gabbie and Jen with their cute girly-meanness that meant they ruled. They were holding hands at the head of the line, playing crack-the-whip. The other, lesser, girls were lined up behind the Barbie-queens, holding on for dear life. Gabbie and Jen raced around the rec room teleposts that held the house up and little girls were flung here and there and everywhere. One of them, Jessica Parkes, a scrawny thing in a polka-dot miniskirt and a LOVE t-shirt, flew off the end of the line and landed on Nathan's Lego pile.

"That's it," Nathan shouted at Gabbie. "This means war. Your friends wreck my Lego, I rip your skinny-tit Barbies limb from limb."

But Gabbie had the ultimate weapon: she could cry on command. Her lip started to tremble and when she opened her mouth, a dainty little-girl wail escaped. "Mom! He's threatening me. It's my birthday and Nathan's trying to ruin it. He says he's going to rip up my Barbies."

Lynette looked at Jack, who hovered in the corner of the rec room reading the Archie comic that had been used to wrap one of Gabbie's presents.

"Jack, you're the dad here. You deal with them." Lynette smiled at Jack like she'd just said something hilarious. She was in perfect mom mode for Gabbie's party, the dream party she had yearned for but had been denied in her own loveless girlhood, but Nathan could tell she was really pissed and when she was really pissed, it was always at Jack.

"It's okay, Mom," Nathan said. "I'm out of here. I'm gone."

"Go to your room," Jack said because he didn't register that Nathan was already on his way there. "If you can't behave you can leave the party."

Nathan could think clearly because his own rage had reached an almost perfect level. The buzz in his head went: I don't want to play in this family any more. I'm consolidating my loans and reinvesting my stock. I'm opting out. He went to his room and slammed the door dramatically because that's what twelve-year-old boys were supposed to do when they were sent to their rooms, but he was no longer out of control. He had a plan.

Nathan took out his school knapsack and dumped everything in it onto the floor. He wouldn't be needing the heavy, dull grade six texts like *Canada Today* and *Math Six*. He wouldn't need his notes on how to conjugate French verbs. He wouldn't need *Old Yeller*, the reading group book for this month. He shoved all these remnants of school drudgery under his bed. In their place in the knapsack he put his wallet with fifteen dollars, his bus pass and his real Air Miles card with his name, Nathan John Grunberg, imprinted on it in raised gold letters. He packed his latest *Youth Entrepreneur* magazine and a *Star Wars* sweatshirt.

Nathan stood on his bed, used both hands to pop the screen out of his bedroom window. He wasn't athletic or strong, but he was skinny and agile and it was easy to wriggle through the narrow opening. Nathan thought about the movie he would one day make about his escape: *Window Slit to Freedom*, perhaps, or *A Boy's Journey to Wealth and Fame*. The climax of every fantasy Nathan had was sweet revenge. He could see his whole future. He imagined how he would give Gabbie a job in his toy factory to show he was a good brother. She could pour the plastic into the moulds for the dolls' heads. The fumes would give her daily migraines and surprisingly cause a rare, untreatable terminal illness. It would be a slow, agonizing death, but Nathan would pay for the best round-the-clock nursing care for Gabbie, and their mom would be moved by his generosity. So moved, she wouldn't mind losing Gabbie so much. She would be so moved that she would declare him the all-time ultimate winner in the mother love contest he had been fighting in and losing since Gabbie was born. Nathan's fantasy broke down there because he couldn't imagine ever winning. No question that his mom would love a dead Gabbie more than a live Nathan.

Lynette's brain said: Bittersweet. Bittersweet. Bittersweet. The little girls were giggling and smearing each other's faces with chocolate ice cream and strawberry blond frosting. They had devoured the head and torso of the Barbie cake. Only those mile-high legs remained. The cake was Lynette's masterpiece. She had made it out of Duncan Hines devil's food cake mix in a special-order Barbie cake pan. The pan cost twenty-three dollars and two proof of purchases from Barbie products and had to be ordered six weeks in advance. The girls were having fun and it was all worth it and she would make it up to Nathan in pirate Lego some time later.

Nathan was Lynette's patient child, not because he had such a sweet disposition, but because he had no choice. For Nathan, childhood was not about surrendering to the moment but about gritting your teeth and waiting to grow up. Gabbie was not patient because she didn't need to be. She was born for childhood the way some people are born to be soldiers or born for the priesthood. She had a little oval birthmark on her chin that glowed when she smiled; someone called it the stamp of delight on her face. She was one of those special people who deserved more than others and would get it. She was a snake charmer in a world of slithering reptiles. She was a dancer who made everyone dance with her. When she was in that trance of make-believe with her little friends, pretending to be Barbie queens, or sisters trapped on a desert island or fashion plate mothers of ill-behaved daughters in need of corrective punishments, or when she was alone, dressing up Latex, the cat, in Cabbage Patch Kids' rompers and feeding him catnip tea from a doll bottle, Lynette envied her childishness. She envied her pleasure. Lynette couldn't remember playing as a child. She was never carefree. She remembered shame. She remembered rage. Childhood for Lynette was getting talked into playing the horse's ass in her siblings' basement theatre production or Lynette getting her head smacked by her father or her brother or her teacher for some inadequacy in her that was never explained. Like it was for Nathan, childhood was a useless place for her to linger, but what choice did anyone have? People didn't even have the pseudo-choice Lynette gave her kids when she used to say when they were smaller, "Red pajamas or blue, Sweetheart? You decide."

Nathan was an expert on city bus routes. Last winter, when he was home sick for a week with a cold that turned into an ear infection, he passed the time by dialing Transit Tom and impersonating serious bus riders. He pretended to be a curmudgeonly old man with urgent appointments in obscure corners of the city. "I'm scheduled to see my open-heart surgeon on Scurfield Crescent at three o'clock. How do I get there from Transcona?" "My wife has passed away. The viewing is at two o'clock at Yaeger's funeral parlour on North Main St." "There is an important jewel auction in South St. Vital at eight o'clock tonight. How do I get there from the Grace Hospital in St. James?" "I am an asthmatic with a long-haired cat to give away. How can I get to the SPCA on Kent Road from Corydon and Stafford and what is the bus fare for cats?"

One of the transit information officers asked Nathan why he wasn't in school. Nathan said he was the famous boy in the bubble, as seen on national television. He was allergic to everything and lacked an immune system to boot. It was hard to say whether she believed him, but she offered to send him a free map of the city with all the bus routes marked and numbered. When the packet came in the mail, Nathan brought the map to school. At recess, while the other kids played soccer or fought over the monkey bars and the swings, he sat with excessive dignity in his *office*, a bare patch of ground between the hardtop and the soccer field, and studied the different routes. He saw himself looking grown up, a valuable member of the community, while the other kids ran around screeching, laughing, kicking and lurching, like the frivolous bunch they were. One day, when he became a leading international toy manufacturer, he would own most of the city, including the bus routes and the schoolyards. These foolish children would work for him, mowing his fields, driving his buses and building his toys. They would proudly tell their co-workers, "I went to school with Nathan G. Grunberg. I always knew he had leadership qualities."

Running away from home was a childish activity and Nathan wanted none of that. What he wanted to do was to catapult himself into the bearable future that was waiting to embrace and celebrate him, waiting almost discernibly somewhere in his aching imagination.

Lynette was standing at the kitchen sink washing the party dishes and singing, "God Loves All the Little Lambees." She had a good voice and her own sweet sound moved her. Downstairs, the girls were still partying. Their happy sounds were a chorus. Lynette pictured Nathan in his room, studying maps, planning strategies. She should have released him. He would have learned his lesson by now, and he had missed the birthday cake, but then the whole nasty business would start up again. She'd saved him a piece of cake, anyway. She couldn't face the jeering, the whining, the crying starting up all over again. Just this one day, she would not go to him. Maybe he would get hungry enough to learn to pray convincingly.

"God loves his little Lambees / He loves them every one / He loves them when they're sunny / He loves them when they're glum." Lynette had trouble making decisions, but singing while washing dishes was an excellent set-up for brewing dangerous thoughts. She couldn't choose between white or dark chocolate. She made most of her important decisions under a thick blanket of distraction. What was hatching in her now was not so much a plan as a deep, mechanical churning. Nestled under the covers in Lynette's brain, the thinking part of her explained, God made us animals and God didn't invent condoms, animals did. Or, if God did invent condoms because he invented everything, he also invented straight pins and the tiny perfect holes they make in foil wrappings and stinky rolled latex.

Lynette dried her hands and then stopped at the top of the stairs and called down to the girls in her sunshine voice: "Is everyone having fun down there?"

"Yes, thank you, Mrs. Grunberg."

"We're fine, Mom!" Gabbie said, keeping her voice sugar and spice like the other girls. Whatever was going on down there, they didn't want Lynette hovering over them with her stretched grin and silly camp songs that used to make them giggle and shriek when she sang them and taught them all the actions. They were busy outgrowing her, forgetting her, and dismissing and hating all adults who still, however meekly and solicitously, thought they were in charge.

Lynette decided to retreat. Midway through the party, Jack had wandered into the bedroom and fallen asleep. Lynette discovered his big, oafish male body lying diagonally across the bed. Under one arm he cradled *What Maisie Knew*, open to his page. His breathing was calm but heavy, like a sickly child's. He hadn't bothered to climb under the covers or to take off his scuffed black leather librarian shoes. Lynette shut the bedroom door and slid out of her light blue terry towel pants and lay down on the bed beside Jack. She gently removed Jack's glasses from the pillow and replaced his book with herself. She wriggled close to him, and they lay there like that, spooning, for a few minutes. Instead of looking at Jack, Lynette watched the minutes on the clock turn over from 2:59 to 3:00. What with the clock clicking over, the faraway sound of the girls squealing from the basement, Nathan in his room waiting to be sprung, there was no space to think about whether it might be easier this way for Jack too, not to have to look at her. He caressed her and squeezed her in his indifferent but gentle style, as if she were warm bread dough, as if every part of her, her face, her hips, her ankles, her soul, her thighs, were equally erotic or not.

Usually when they made love, Lynette bartered for some small declaration of fondness, some specificity of attraction. Jack had to say her name at least. Lynette wasn't required to speak, only to make convincing noises that could be interpreted as pleasure. Sometimes his declarations were too vague ("I love doing this. I need this"). This time, Lynette felt generous and in love. She imagined she was cheating on Jack by making love to Jack's God-fearing, sexually knowledgeable, perfectly confident clone. The fantasy was so arousing that she came before he did without needing him to whisper *love bug, I love you*, or other magic words.

In the end, Nathan took the familiar number sixty Pembina bus downtown. He waited for it nervously, slouching against the glass pane of the bus shack, not because today he was a boy unaccountably at large in frozen-dog Winnipeg but out of habit. When he was out in the world, he was used to being sneered at and bullied. He was the kind of kid teenagers took cotton candy from if they spotted him alone in a lineup at the Red River Ex. His bony knees and jutting shoulder blades and his serious look of oblivious self-righteousness reminded them of their worst selves. They loved to take out their self-loathing on Nathan. Once he was on the bus without incident, he relaxed into his seat, silently naming the side streets as they glided by and imagining the driver's potential pride and gratitude at having Nathan Grunberg, future owner of all public transportation, on her bus.

After a few minutes, a woman with bloated eyes and red, raw skin got on the bus with her squalling brood of small children in tow. She was wearing a grey-stained, puffy parka over a timeless stretch pantsuit. Nathan thought of the saggy, baggy elephant from the Golden books. Nathan's mother had the same kind of pantsuits, but they were a girlish size small. Nathan's mother bought them new at Saan and gave them to the church second-hand store when they got *pilly* from the washing machine. Lynette's clothes had a magical crispness to them and a clean smell that this woman's lacked.

The mother and her baby, a bloated, snotty-nosed, drooling mass in pink fleece, squeezed in next to Nathan. She directed the three other kids to the seat across the aisle. Except for the baby, who whined and moaned while excreting various juices, the children were all shell-shocked-expressionless and mute. The mother's indifference to her children and the world included Nathan. He was the dam between her and the window and her heaving body flowed menacingly against his. He was claustrophobic and found himself panting gently and wishing the bus driver Godspeed, but he also felt snug with the cold metal of the bus window on one side and the pillowy plastic of the diaper bag sticking to his cheek and arm. He couldn't move and didn't dare try. The mother had no sharp edges. She was like a warm, sticky pool spreading out and absorbing him. Strange how Nathan John Grunberg, youth entrepreneur and future world leader, partly liked the feeling of disappearing into this sweaty monster of a woman. The smell of her clothes, her body and her baby's spit-up made him feel slightly dizzy and nauseous, but the woman's indifferent capture of all his personal space made him feel both safe and suffocated. Then the baby started crying and coughing and really threw up. Some of the puke landed on Nathan. He lurched, gagged and managed to pull on the cord to signal the bus driver to let him off. The woman ignored him and mechanically pulled a rag from her sleeve and rubbed it on the baby's face. "Mental note," Nathan silently told his pretend high-tech miniature Dictaphone: "1. Never have children. 2. Provide special family zones on buses and special business class seats for important businessmen." The bus was pulling up to Graham Avenue and Smith Street. Mercifully, Earth Smother and her brood were getting off too.

Jack reached for Lynette, but she was already dressed and back in the kitchen. He could hear cupboards slamming. That was one of her things—slamming cupboard doors. She did it when she needed to let the inner turmoil out. When Nathan was a baby and she and Jack had been arguing about something in the car—money, God, or whether Jack went out to too many movies—she would bring Nathan in from the car in his car seat and put him on the counter. Nathan would be sleeping inside his bunting and snug car seat straps and she would say, "Let me make us some coffee, Honey, and we'll talk this thing out." She was the calm, reasonable one with that go-the-distance smile, but then, each time she opened a cupboard door, she would slam it so hard the porch shook. In a few moments, Nathan would be wailing. She would pick him up and comfort him, making elaborate soothing gestures that only made him more furious. She would look at Jack as though he had poisoned the baby. There was no possibility of talking, Jack reasoned, and he retreated from the racket and his wife and child's unhappiness. He would make himself inconspicuous on the living room couch or on his bed, open his book, find his place and slide deep under the waters of the text without even needing to first take a breath.

On the afternoon of Gabbie's ninth birthday, lying in bed feeling relaxed and fleetingly hopeful after napus interruptus, Jack was not tempted to get up, go into the kitchen and try to talk out what the cupboard-slamming was all about. He had a brief, horrifying realization that their passion was sans plastic wrap—no condom, no protection—and quickly put his clothes on and found himself in his book. Phrases like *right time of the month* and *rhythm method* fluttered through his consciousness, but he had never known the details of these female secrets. He felt ashamed, not that his wife was so quickly separate from him after lovemaking, not that her anger must symbolize some flaw in him, but at his foolishness at not using birth control. His own father, a work-obsessed miser of a gentleman who nevertheless grew his hair in 1968 and often lamented aloud that he had not been young enough to enjoy the free love movement of the sixties, would never have made such a mistake. Jack's father had survived the Depression. He was vigilant. Jack smoothed out the blankets and sat at the side of the bed, hunched over to the place in *What Maisie Knew* where James shows that Maisie knew far too much about grown-up jealousy, pettiness, indifference and cruelty.

Gabbie and Lynette were at the door handing out grab bags. "Thank you for coming to my party." "Bye. Thanks." "Bye." They gave out Barbie grab bags and each one contained a Wunderbar, banana-shaped barrettes, flower lick-em tattoos and a soother pop ring. It was a good party even though Jen won Spin the Bottle and Gabbie had to kiss Jessica. She had kissed her hard and fast like a punch and Jessica had cried and said her teeth hurt. But Jen stuck up for Gabbie because they were best friends and because it was Gabbie's party. "It's not our fault you've got those big beaver teeth," Jen told Jessica. "You tell and we all say it was your idea." Jessica quivered but didn't crumble and Gabbie got a free spin.

Nathan sat with the chess players at the downtown library, his dad's library, a place he knew well enough to feel comfortably anonymous. His dad was at home now because it was Saturday and Gabbie's birthday party. People walking by might think he was Josh from the movie *Searching for Bobby Fischer*, but no one stopped to gawk. He sat next to Dale, an unemployed thirty-something adolescent id-sav in the required black-rimmed glasses and a stained, grey Adidas track suit. Dale was playing speed chess with Anthony Chochinov, the Methuselah of the Winnipeg chess scene. Choch was a former grand master and rumoured to have coached Kasparov when they were both Russian teens.

Nathan wasn't interested in the details of chess, the openings and endgames and the obsessive concentration required to be a real player, but he liked the tone of the game, especially speed chess: black against white; check, slam the clock, evade, slam the clock, check/clock, check/clock, checkmate.

By refusing all invitations to play, he maintained his mysterious kid/champion-to-be status.

Whenever Choch made a move, which was often in speed chess, he said something profound, meant to help Nathan in his development as a chess player and as a human being. "The clock. She's out to get you. Never forget that. The clock; she's your enemy."

Nathan responded with wisdom of his own, usually off topic. "In a few years, I'm going to run this town. I've got the vision. I've got the drive and I've got the patience." He would have added, And my dad's an important investment banker, but the chess players at the library might have known his dad was a security guard there.

Dale grunted and wiped his mouth with his sleeve. "Checkmate," he said and stopped both sides of the clock with the palm of his hand. "Hey, kid, I'll play ya for a Mars bar."

"Naw, I don't gamble," Nathan said

"You don't gamble, you don't live," Choch said.

"You don't gamble, you don't lose," Dale snickered.

"That's good advice for the kid," Choch said and actually winked at Nathan, his wrinkled lid dissolving into infinite ripples.

He is kind, Nathan thought, but repulsive. He wants to drool his old man's wisdom on me before it dries up completely. Nathan was afraid Choch might seize up and die in mid-platitude.

Dale and Choch played a few more rounds and Nathan stood up and wandered over to the magazine section. He was reading *Fortune* when he was startled by Dale's reflexively accusatory voice.

"You won't get rich reading about it, kid." He gave Nathan what was supposed to be a playful punch in the arm, but it had force to it and Nathan jumped back.

"Yeah, well," Nathan said, rubbing his arm. He thought about going home. He wasn't mad any more and he imagined his mother crying and praying, calling up all her church friends to come over and wail and pray and declare a miracle when he finally showed up. He imagined his father, trembling with anxiety, too sick with worry even to read a magazine. Nathan knew this fantasy was extreme—his father read when he was relaxed and read more when he was tense. There was no time that his father did not have an urgent appointment with the pages of a book. Still, Nathan had made his parents suffer enough.

"Come over to my house and I'll show you my vinyl." When Dale said *vinyl*, he lurched forward and put his face close to Nathan's. He said *vinyl* the way King Midas must have said *gold*; the way Nathan said *bus routes*.

"Okay," Nathan said, the lure of vinyl temporarily overruling the lure of home.

As they walked to Dale's Kennedy Street basement suite, Nathan explained his plans for the city. "This is where the sky bus route will be. It'll go right through Eaton's and the Bay. You won't even have to go outside."

Dale was unmoved. "Do you even play chess?" he demanded.

Nathan soldiered on. "People will object at first, mainly to the cost, but it's like, 'If you build it, they will come.' Once we have the sky train and the tunnels, they'll wonder how they ever lived without it."

"Nathan's way or the highway," Dale said, showing he was at least half listening. "I smoked Choch today," he added. "That senile old fart."

All Gabbie's friends were gone and she was whirling into despair. Throughout the house were signs of the wreckage of the party: footless legs of a chocolate Barbie cake in the kitchen, Lego, game pieces, and old doll parts strewn across the rec room. The presents that looked so tantalizingly more than she deserved when they were wrapped in pretty paper and ribbons and piled high on the dining room table looked meagre and dull now that they were opened and spread out across the living room carpet. Gabbie was literally whirling, doing a combination of ballet and kung fu moves through the house. She had already said no to her mother's offer of a game of cards or starting a jigsaw puzzle. She didn't just say "No," she said, "That's stupid. It's my birthday. Don't you even care that it's my birthday?"

Lynette said, "Of course, I care. Didn't you like your party, Sugar?"

Gabbie lied and said, "No, I hated it. Nathan ruined it like he ruins everything," And then she ran off to do her fighting dance.

Lynette had retreated into the kitchen and started slamming cupboard doors. Now Gabbie's misery was compounded by her guilt about being mean to her mother and the feeling in the pit of her stomach that she always had when she knew Mom was about to blow. She pirouetted and punched her way to Nathan's room. With a quick, graceful spin she was up in the air, kicking the door to his room open.

She saw his schoolbooks on the floor, his bed with the ugly boyish plaid comforter crumpled and exposing faded Mickey Mouse sheets, but no Nathan. How strange. How exciting. Nathan had disappeared. Was it because Gabbie had wished it? No, it couldn't be, Gabbie thought. She had wished him invisible, vamoosed, never born, away, so many times before and he always stubbornly stuck around. Today, she'd only thought about him a little bit. True, he had lunged at one of her friends and tried to hijack her birthday party with his lonely, left out "Mom, what about me" tactics, but today, none of his tricks had paid off. Today, Gabbie had been so thoroughly victorious that her anger at Nathan was more reflexive than heartfelt.

Gabbie looked around the room and saw that the window was open. The idea of Nathan running away infuriated Gabbie the way his habit of cheating at Monopoly or any other game did. She was so mad she started grinding her teeth and her fingers started twitching. She herself had run away several times, but only as far as the bare spot of ground under the Andersons' pine tree at the end of the block. When Gabbie ran away, she always announced her intentions, several times if her parents were distracted, and then slammed the front door for emphasis. Her kind of running away was part of a dialogue, not like what it appeared Nathan had done, which was to opt out completely—to break the rules of the game of family. As Gabbie was storming out, her mother would be shouting at her, keeping her tethered: "Do you think you can run away from God?" or "Don't think you'll be missed, Miss" or "At least put a jacket on." When Gabbie came back, Mom would hug her and say, "Look what the kitty dragged in," or "Praise be to God; the child is returned to us." She would make her hot chocolate with miniature coloured marshmallows and if the whole incident had been Nathan's fault, if he had been sneering at her or torturing her dolls or playing Nerf sniper against her unwitting friends, he wouldn't get any hot chocolate or, for a minor offense, no marshmallows.

How could Nathan run away, and what sort of reward would he get when he returned? Gabbie knew she should tell her parents Nathan was gone, but first spent a little time inspecting his room. To Gabbie, the room was nothing but dweebo-dweeb. She wished she had found something in the room that could make her look up to him and want to root for him, but everything in the den of Nathan reminded Gabbie of her brother's square-headed desire to torture her or at best embarrass her. The crummy Lego airport he'd designed himself and sent a photograph of to the Lego company was gathering dust on top of his dresser. Who ever heard of a square airplane? No wonder he had never heard back from Lego headquarters. Gabbie fingered Nathan's stack of *Star Wars* comics and flipped through the pages of one, but the blue background and silver steel-faced characters and the tiny serious words in heavy square balloons didn't interest her. She pulled some books out of the bookshelf, but there was nothing hidden behind them. Even Nathan's frog bank, made by Aunt Andie when he was three, made no inviting sound when she rattled it. He must have taken the good stuff with him. In a moment of inspiration, Gabbie closed the window and fastened the latch, effectively destroying Nathan's chances of not getting caught whenever he came crawling back. Then she went to watch television and wait for him to come home.

Dale's apartment smelled like mouldy bread. In the main room, there was nothing but a squishy grey carpet that might have once been any colour in the rainbow and records, records, records. One wall had square shelves like school cubbyholes stacked with recoreds and there were records lining the floor along each of the other walls. The room was barely navigable because of the records stacked in piles a foot high throughout the remaining floor space. There was nowhere to sit except on the records themselves. Nathan tried to sit on one pile but Dale yanked him up. "That's my Rat Pack collection, you dimbo."

Nathan was unimpressed. His first apartment would be a penthouse. He already had plans to make an offer they couldn't refuse on the revolving restaurant on top of Fort Garry Place. He would redecorate with grey, sleek, sharp-edged furniture, a Star Ship Enterprise and original, framed, signed comic book prints on the walls. Modern, atonal music would be piped in over a state-of-the-art speaker system. All Dale had on the walls was a creased poster of a half-naked biker chick. She wore a leather bikini and had a tattoo of a rat peeking out of a black leather triangle on one of her balloon breasts.

Dale was rocking back and forth, grinning like he'd just pulled the curtain on door number three to reveal a new Cadillac.

"Wow," Nathan said. "Quite a lot of records."

"A shitload," Dale said, turning red from modesty. "Come on. I'll show you the pleasure den." The pleasure den was the bedroom, which was about the size of a large walk-in closet. It was big enough to hold Dale's single bed and his turntable and a small night table with a chess set on it. On the wall was another biker chick, this one bending over, showing off the tattoo on her rear. The tattoo said *Lick-a-Dick* in girly handwriting, and showed a Smartie-red mouth opening for what Nathan thought was a popsicle.

Nathan had no choice but to sit on the bed and watch Dale fondle records and play selections for him. It occurred to Nathan that he was a child alone with a very strange adult who might want to do unspeakable things to him. Nathan should have been afraid of Dale and his pleasure den, but Dale didn't care about anything but chess and the vinyl disks he owned. Dale was so focussed on his albums, so knowledgeable about them, that he talked on as if he was giving a lecture he had given many times before. Nathan listened intently for the point in Dale's monologue where the records were revealed as bait and Dale revealed his true, sordid, sadistic intentions. Dale slid a Billie Holiday album out of its plastic cover. "Look at this baby. Not a scratch on her; never been played."

"Wow. Are you going to play it?"

Dale scowled at Nathan like he had just hung his queen in a chess tournament. "My God, you're stupid, kid," he said, sliding the record back into its pristine sleeve and putting it well out of Nathan's reach.

Whatever Dale might do to Nathan was not going to be the sort of thing that happens to children who run away from home, children who live on the streets. Dale was creepy and weird, but apparently not intent on destroying Nathan's innocence.

In the end, all that happened was that Dale talked and played cuts for practically an hour until Nathan had a sore back from sitting and pretending to listen, though he realized that listening wasn't really required. Dale was his own best audience. When Nathan finally stood up and said he really had to go home now, Dale led him to a pantry attached to his kitchen, which had a small freezer. Nathan thought, this is it. He braced himself for Dale to reveal the body parts carefully stacked in the freezer—Dale's dead parents' livers and kidneys, carefully dated and labelled—but instead, Dale pulled out a five-kilogram bag of crinkle-cut McCain fries. "Only 5% Fat!" the label gloated. Nathan understood that Dale wanted him to take the bag as a parting gift.

"You don't have to," Nathan said.

"No. No. I want to," Dale answered, gingerly placing the cold plastic sack in Nathan's arms.

"That's a lot of fries. It probably wouldn't be good for me to eat that much," Nathan said and instantly regretted the suggestion that weight mattered. He was a skinny pre-acne kid and Dale's sweatsuit could only hide so much of medicated-welfare-nerd post-adolescent bloat.

"Yeah, well," Dale said. "They're baked, not fried. I like to put them in soup."

If Nathan was going to leave and make it home before dark, he would have to take the sack of fries with him. "Thanks a lot, Dale. I had a good time," Nathan said, hugging the cold plastic sack against his sweatshirt. It was the standard goodbye line his mom taught him for those rare play dates with other kids and he was grateful to have the words automatically available here and for future encounters.

"Yeah, see you around, kid. You still owe me a game of chess."

Nathan abandoned the sack of fries on the rear seat of the bus. Assuming Dale hadn't poisoned them, some homeless or really poor person might find them useful. Right now it was time for Nathan to go back home where he could safely wait out the rest of his childhood.

"Gabbie, what have you done with your brother?" Lynette yelled over the sounds of *Scooby-Doo* emanating from the television set. "Jack, she's killed him. It's finally over."

Luckily for Gabbie, she could out-hysteric Lynette any day. She was especially annoyed that she would have to miss the inevitable discovery that what seemed like real magic evil in Scooby-ville was just hocus pocus, shenanigans. On *Scooby-Doo*, there is an inane but reassuring explanation for everything.

Jack paced wildly in front of the television alternating between comforting lines to Lynette-such as: "Nine-year-olds aren't killers." "How long has he been gone?" "Let's talk this through."—and repeatedly to Gabbie: "What do you know about this? Spill."

Gabbie hurled her head back and started smacking it on the back of the couch. She kicked her feet wildly at the coffee table. "It's still my birthday. What kind of people are you? I hate you. I hate you forever."

Everyone was hysterical—sobbing and shrieking; accusing and blaming. Lynette was back to slamming cupboard doors. Jack was smacking his fist into his palm like a chimp while he paced. Gabbie was the loudest and her tears the most copious. "I didn't kill him—you did. You two psycho parents. I'm reporting you to Children's Aid."

At this moment, Nathan made his entrance. He had to slam the front door to get everyone's attention. They all stopped and stared at him like he was the Baby Jesus on a Harley. It was a sitcom moment and it would have been wonderful if they could cut to a commercial after a tearful reunion and sentimental promises all around, but Nathan was an eleven-year-old with what his grandmother called a long head. He knew he had at least seven more years to last here. To fortify himself, Nathan imagined staring them down and saying quietly but with irrevocable force: "You're fired. You're all fired. You have twenty minutes to pack your things and get out." Instead, he tried for a withered, childish look and said, "Hi, Mom. Hi, Dad. Here I am. I'm okay. There's nothing to worry about."

The crisis was deflated. They all felt guilty, as if they had walked away from a crime scene without getting caught, but also angry because the others had not been caught or punished for their part in things. Mom gave Nathan a tight hug and he stood there, surrounded by her for as long as he could bear. She released him and they all retreated to their corners. Jack went to the couch and cracked open *What Maisie Knew*. Gabbie went to the basement to assess her birthday haul. She called Jen on the phone to plan a sleepover at Jen's house for the next day. Nathan went to his room to put things back in their proper place. Lynette went into the bathroom and locked the door. She examined an ugly black hair on a mole on her neck that had sprouted again and needed to be tweezed. She washed her hands and her face and checked the state of her teeth. We're all all right, she thought. For the moment, Praise Jesus, we're all all right.

Down the Rabbit Hole

One morning when Nathan and Gabbie were at school, Lynette went out to the Saan store and bought pale pink leggings and a black and pink stretch top with geometric shapes on its various ruffles. Even at $16.99, it was a silly outfit for anyone who wasn't deeply and deliriously pregnant. Lynette took the outfit home and hid it in the bottom of her sweater drawer. First she took the tags off and rumpled it so it would seem as though it had always been in the sweater drawer, not some sudden but premeditated purchase that would reveal Lynette's criminal nature, but a forgotten, necessary, prudent object from the past, which had been carefully preserved in the unlikely surprising event that it was needed. Like now.

It had been only twenty-three days. Too soon for a pregnancy test. The kids came home from school, fought, watched *Three's Company* and *Family Ties*, stared achingly at their homework, and somehow got through dinner with Jack slurping spaghetti, his head at a precarious angle so he could ingest and read the magazine balanced on his knee. At bedtime, Gabbie panicked because her homework wasn't done. She cried and said it just wasn't possible for a nine-year-old to do all that. "What are they trying to do? Destroy childhood? I'm just a kid."

Lynette wrote a note to the teacher saying that Gabbie was excused from finishing her homework because it was absurd to make an innocent young girl who does the best she can slave away all evening and still go to bed with a feeling of doom and a perhaps permanent sense of failure. "Are you trying to eliminate childhood altogether?" she wrote. "It seems that way to us." And she signed the note Dr. and Mrs. Jack Grunberg because Jack had finished his PhD even if he did work as a library security guard.

Gabbie said her prayers. "Thank you Jesus for keeping Mommy and Daddy and Dumb Blockhead Nathan safe. Thank you especially for cuddly Mommy who loves me best. Amen." And she gave Lynette the kind of hug that makes motherhood worthwhile.

Then Lynette went into Nathan's room. He told her he prayed privately now and she let him get away with it, not because she didn't want to know what was in his head, but because she wasn't going to be the kind of parent who rammed Jesus down her kids' throats. Nathan still let her lie down with him as she had done since he was a baby. He let her rub his back and hum a lullaby. Now that he was older, he sometimes flinched at her first touch, but then he relaxed into it. Sometimes he wanted to talk, but always about other people or the imagined future, never about himself. His day at school was always fine. If she asked if the other kids teased him, he would say, "I can stand it," in a martyr voice that didn't tell her anything at all. If another kid was humiliated at school, he would tell her about it in a tone of serious glee. "They told Tommy Ryan that Melanie had a crush on him and to meet her at the monkey bars at second recess. He went out and stood there the whole recess while Melanie and her friends hid in the girls' bathroom. When the bell rang, he still stood there with a look on his face like, 'There must be some mistake. I have an appointment.' The recess monitor had to go back outside and drag him in and I think he got a detention."

"Poor Tommy. Why are children so mean?" Lynette said, lying beside Nathan, rubbing a figure eight on his back.

"Poor Tommy," Nathan said, his voice vibrating with scorn. "Why is he such a moron?"

"Poor Nathan. Poor baby," Lynette cooed in Nathan's ear.

"No. It's poor stupid Tommy," Nathan corrected her, but he let her breathe on him and treat him like a child even though it made him feel weak and ashamed because this bedtime was the time, the only time since Gabbie was born, that he had his mom all to himself and he wasn't ready to give that up. They had read *The Secret Garden* in school last year and he still thought his mom treated him like Colin's father had treated Colin, the boy in the story who used a wheelchair and screamed for treats from his bed because he had been taught to believe he was an invalid even though he was perfectly fine. As Nathan drifted off to sleep, he thought he heard her whispering, "Can't. Can't. Can't. Never ever. Never ever." He dreamed he sat up in bed and his legs felt like lead and he couldn't get up. He shouted, "I'm not gonna live to grow up. I'm not even gonna live to grow up." His mother drifted in, eyes full of sleep and looking like a fairy princess in her white embroidered nightgown. Nathan felt her hands on his shoulders and her warm breath in his ear: "Poor thing. My poor, poor thing. Don't worry, Natey. You'll always be my baby."

Every Saturday afternoon for three weeks after the birthday party, Jack and Lynette made love while the kids were loose in the house. The illicitness of it made Jack wild. He took Lynette's sudden, surprising passion as a sign that his patience was finally paying off. Everyone goes through rough patches when they first have kids. Things were finally getting on to an even keel again. Now that the kids were older, now that there was some predictability in life again, now they could become the family they imagined themselves worthy of being. Jack and Lynette ignored sounds of chaos coming from the rec room. "Let the kids sort this one out for themselves," Lynette said, already naked and slipping into bed beside him. For the first time since Nathan was born, she was able to put Jack first and give the kids the space they needed to grow up healthy. Jack suspected and his mother often articulated that all Nathan's problems were related to Lynette's hovering. When Jack was a kid, parents didn't even know where their kids were most of the time. His mother baked cookies and went to school band concerts and put on a pretty good holiday meal, but that was about it. "I brought you into the world," she would say, half seriously whenever Jack or his sisters whined or misbehaved. "Haven't I done enough?"

Lynette gingerly lifted Jack's book out of his hands and put it on the bedside table. She straddled him and held his hands and looked at him square in the face. This was so far from the tepid groping in the dark of the past how many years. "I love you," he said without prompting. "You're still the girl I fell in love with in Mrs. Evan's history class." They were both meticulous about the condom, as though precision now would make up for their earlier carelessness.

Lynette couldn't believe how easy it was to find the mood.

"Permission to enter," Jack said in a robotic voice.

"Permission denied. Permission denied. Permission granted."

For years, sex had been like building a multi-storeyed house of cards. One misplaced breath, one slip and the whole prospect of pleasure collapsed in a heap. Now, suddenly, inexplicably, sex was relaxed, fun and unconditional. It must be God's will, Lynette thought and Jack would have been thinking too if he had been thinking anything at that moment.

Gabbie's feet thundered up the basement stairs and down the hall. She hurled herself against the door. "I need you, Mommy. I need you right now."

"One minute, Baby," Lynette said, digging her fingernails into Jack's back as a signal that he didn't have to hold back. Jack climaxed while Gabbie threw herself against the door with such force that it was a miracle she didn't injure herself or at least damage the door. Her desperation tired her out, though, and by the time they were dressed and opened the door, Gabbie was asleep on the carpet in the hallway, her face still wet with tears.

Since running away and getting away with it, Nathan found family life more tolerable. Now he had a choice. He could leave any time he wanted to, but for the moment, he chose to stay. He took to phoning airlines and inquiring into the price of tickets to what seemed to him exotic locales like Washington, DC and Calgary, Alberta. Instead of choking his sister when she drove him nuts, two times out of three, he would just walk away and get on the phone and start making reservations. Nathan's newly found calm caused Gabbie to regress back to the terrible twos. She had violent fits of rage that weren't overtly Nathan's fault. Maybe Nathan's recently acquired stainless steel demeanour was what it would feel like to be a grown-up—coolly, distantly, almost sympathetically watching people hurl dishes, slam doors, rage, terrorize and otherwise shame themselves while you sat back in the state his father called "half-chagrined." It was all about taking the high road. You were calm. You were in control. You were grudgingly respected. You wore a suit and tie. You ruled. Nathan held this promise of adult life in front of him like a carrot in front of a mule, hoping it could entice him through the next seven-and-a-half excruciating years of childhood.

Lynette had wasted $13.95 on a home pregnancy test. Enough for a small package of disposable diapers, or for a family of four to eat at McDonald's. She sat on the toilet in the basement bathroom and watched for the second blue line to appear on the tester stick. The test was positive, as Lynette knew it would be. Already she had the vague, overfull feeling most of the time that would soon turn into real nausea and then full-out morning sickness. She had the fatigue too—she could nap anytime, anywhere—and her breasts felt all tingly and tender like they were about to bloom any day. She sat there, massaging her abdomen, but it was soft and unmiraculous, as it had remained since Gabbie's birth. The pregnancy was real, but still more of an idea than a solid, immovable object.

She was ecstatic, but terrified. Jack would be appalled, possibly enraged, but definitely not overjoyed. At least not at first. Later, so her script went, he would see that this child was inevitable, necessary and delightful. She thought of calling her sister Andie in Vancouver, to tell her the news. She needed to speak it out loud. But then she thought of Andie's meagre one daughter, little Eva, who had allergies, possibly a learning disability, and a dense, half-cocked expression on her pale little face, and Lynette felt it would be like bragging to tell Andie. The person she most wanted to tell was Ann-Marie, who taught Sunday school at the church and volunteered as a doula at home births. Ann-Marie had four children, all blond and chubby and with cheeks as red as hardened alcoholics'. She dressed them in Holly Hobbie-style clothes that she must have made herself or received as hand-me-downs from the Hutterites. The only word for Ann-Marie's children was *strapping*. Around Ann-Marie, Lynette was ashamed of her skinny, ill-tempered *artistic* children. Lynette's family was a dry wasteland and Ann-Marie's a garden.

"Hi, Ann-Marie, it's me." Lynette compulsively delayed identifying herself on the phone, a habit that had become a heated topic during Jack and Lynette's church-sponsored Explore and Celebrate Your Marriage retreat several years ago.

"Oh, hi," Ann-Marie said, as if she had no idea who was on the other end of the line.

"I've got the most exciting news," Lynette said. "And you're the person I wanted to tell first."

"I'm sorry, who is this?" Ann-Marie said.

"It's nobody. Nobody at all. Nobody important," Lynette said, with her signature laugh, which always made Jack feel both superior and sorry for her. Lynette slammed down the phone as Ann-Marie was starting to say, "Lynette, is that you?"

Lynette retreated to the bathroom, the one carefully enclosed space in the world that knew everything about her. She sat on the toilet and peed and cried and wondered how it could be that Ann-Marie was so good at everything, even meanness. She pulled the plastic pregnancy test stick out of the garbage and looked at it. The two blue lines were still there. Most certainly. At this point, the pregnancy didn't seem real. It was like having an imaginary friend you want to play with, but when you do, your parents mock you and call you a liar and a freak for talking to yourself. Lynette put cold water on her face and washed her hands and went back to the bedroom and called her sister Andie.

"Hey, Andie. It's me."

"Is there something wrong?"

"No, not at all. You'll never believe this, Andie," Lynette said with a giggle rising up in her throat.

Andie steadied herself for one of the three possible things Lynette might say: "I'm really married to Jesus now," or "Jack's finally agreed that we can move back home," or, the soap opera one, "I'm pregnant." When Lynette picked door number three, Andie exhaled in relief. "That's great. I mean. I think. Really? Are you totally sure?"

"Isn't it a miracle?" Lynette said. She wasn't going to spare Andie any of the joy of the moment of discovery. If Andie was envious, she could just swallow it. They were sisters, after all, and this was Lynette's moment. The conversation proceeded as if following a script. They talked about how Lynette was feeling, how far along she was, when she would tell the kids, baby names (maybe Eli for a boy or Sierra for a girl), whether Andie could send some of her old maternity clothes. Did she plan on having amnio this time? There was no talk about Andie's work, her home renovations, her highly placed friends.

When they hung up, Lynette was floating. She was at the beginning of a beautiful dream. It didn't matter that somewhere under the surface, Lynette knew what Andie would say to her husband Louis that night. "Hasn't she heard of birth control?" she would ask. "Why is it some people just breed like rabbits? She didn't say what Jack thought about it and I was afraid to ask. I bet this one finishes them off." Lynette knew Andie was thinking all these things and worse, but she could choose not to let it ruin her mood. Life is full of choices. Lynette's choice was temporary euphoria, which held all through Nathan and Gabbie coming home from school, Gabbie with a nosebleed, sobbing about stains on her Sassy Girl t-shirt and Nathan jeering at Gabbie to make it all worse. It held through Nathan's wide-eyed, blank, silent response to her questions about school. "Do you have homework?" "Did you have gym?" "Did anyone hurt you today?" "Do you act like a goddamn deaf mute at school too?" "No wonder the kids pick on you, Nathan, for heaven sakes." Lynette covered her hand with her mouth. She hadn't really said that to Nathan. The evidence was that he was now slouching on the couch, eating a box of Oreos and watching *Three's Company*. He was immune to her, anyway.

"Come on, Gabbie, change your shirt and let's make chocolate chip cookies."

"Mmmmmm. Cookies. Can I eat some of the dough?"

"You can have a spoonful."

Jack should have known Lynette was pregnant long before she told him. The most glaring sign was that she had become Suzy Homemaker, baking treats and lighting sweet-smelling candles in the bathroom. She was making *couple time* a priority. Jack knew that all this serenity was too good to last. He knew he was getting only a brief reprieve and that very soon he would again be bludgeoned with adult responsibility and made to face his inadequacies as a responsible grown-up. He made an unconscious decision not to be angry or suspicious; not to flee or retreat any more than he had to for sanity and to ride Lynette's good-time, happy-family wave until it broke on him and tossed his lifeless corpse onto the beach. Call it opportunism or call it Zen, but for once, Jack was living in the present tense.

There was no excuse for the way he behaved when she finally told him. She was already three months gone and wearing nothing but spandex clothes. "Jack," she said one night after they had made love and after he had stroked her stretched midsection with the absence of recognition that was his trademark. "Jack, look at this cute little bear and the booties Andie sent us." Lynette held up a light green terry towel bear and a pair of impossibly small knitted baby booties.

It was a test. What would it take to make Jack twig? Would he think the booties were for the bear and the bear was for Gabbie? No matter that Gabbie had given up teddy bears once and for all at the age of three, when she discovered Barbies. Lynette's changing body, her abstinence from coffee and wine, her soda crackers on the night stand, her new wardrobe of shifts and stretch pants, her recent notable serenity and, most glaring of all, her sudden love of sex—none of it had clued Jack in. It was like she was screaming it at him and he was plugging his ears. He refused to pay attention and it couldn't be her fault if he didn't want to know.

None of the obvious signals made it through to Jack. Even the persistent ache in his own gut that could only be a by-product of his over-functioning repression machine didn't wake him up. But green, hand-knitted booties. He was not a stupid man. He pulled away from Lynette and sat on the edge of the bed. He was a grown man, practically middle-aged, and naked except for his socks. Lynette inched close to him and reached her arm around his torso. He removed her arm, not harshly, but not gently, either. Then he was on his feet, pacing. His face was red and even though naked men in their socks should feel vulnerable and silly, he just felt volcanic.

"Lynette, there cannot be another child. There is not another child. There will not be another child."

Lynette had expected this kind of initial response. When Jack asserted himself, he always overdid it. "You're just like the Wizard of Oz, always blowing smoke and sounding grand and fierce to cover up for all you don't understand," she told him. He responded, not in words, but in dying animal sounds, not at all becoming to a naked library security guard.

Lynette held out Jack's boxer shorts for him. She said, as if she were reasoning with a very stubborn three-year-old, "There will be another child, your child. You and I will love this child as much as we love Gabbie and Nathan. Stop this foolishness and put on your shorts."

"Awoooo. Aawoooo. Aah. Aah. Aah," Jack said.

Lynette lay in the bed with her hand massaging her belly. "Shhhh. The baby can hear everything you say. The first words you speak to him are words of hate. I can't even believe you."

This had some effect and Jack shut up and put on his shorts. Lynette held the blanket open and Jack fell back into bed. She drew his hand down to her abdomen, not yet ballooning, but already taut like a pigskin drum. Jack was crying and saying over and over, "Let this be a dream. Let this be a dream."

"It is a dream, Sweetie. A beautiful, wonderful dream."

Nathan's mother was getting fat and sleeping all the time. His sister was the same old same old princess who wore her ballet tutu to school in the middle of January with bare legs and white leather moccasins instead of boots. On the moccasins she had drawn tulips and happy faces in pink and purple and green marker. She looked like a freak, but Nathan had problems of his own. His doctor said he was eighty percent through puberty and he was not quite twelve years old. He had hair in places that shouldn't be. His child body was morphing into a monster man's. His shoes were size ten and a half. Last year they were seven.

To deal with things, Nathan was starting his own business. He collected rocks and polished them in his rock tumbler that his Auntie Andie gave him last Christmas. It took drive to find rocks to polish in the winter but he had plenty of drive. He also had time at recess at school to dig up parts of the playground and the school's front garden where the best rocks were. Nathan had a "Ravishing Rocks" stand at the end of their block, but so far only pity customers, no serious customers. Actually, so far the only customers were his mom and dad and Darren, a high school boy who lived on their bay. Darren wanted a rock to throw through his garage window because he had locked himself out and it was about twenty below zero. If another person shuffled by and, instead of buying suggested, "How about a lemonade stand?" Nathan might just go ballistic on him. First of all, it was unbearably cold, the wind was up and even though it was only four o'clock, the sun had already set. He would have had to sell frozen lemonade. Who would want that in the cold, dark night? Nathan thought, disgusted at the general lack of marketing savvy in his neighbourhood.

By the time the street lights flipped on at five o'clock,

Nathan's hands felt like solid blocks—no moving digits—so he packed up his wares and went inside. His mother should have been in the kitchen listening to CJOB's evangelical show, *God Is Right Here*, and making dinner, but she was in her room with the door shut. Once Nathan walked in on her in her room and she was in her underwear and bra, on her knees, praying, she said, but he felt like it was that weird ball that was now her stomach she was praying to. She was rubbing it and her belly button stuck out like some freakish deformed thumb. Nathan was hungry but he wasn't going to risk going in there again.

Gabbie was on the couch in the living room, watching *Family Ties* and eating Ritz crackers from the box. She was also on the phone with Jessica, talking about how Clarissa was such a wannabe, how she even tried to dress like Gabbie even though she was fat and needed a bra but refused to wear the one her mother bought her except on gym days when she had to change in front of the other girls. Other days, Nathan would have gone in and sat with her and watched the show. He loved that show. Alex with his hyper voice and little business suit and clean-cut ambition was as close as it came to a role model for Nathan. Today, he couldn't stomach Gabbie and her trivial little-girl concerns.

"Hey fuckface," he said to her, making a swipe for the box of Ritz. "You're gonna be as fat as Melissa Manders if you keep eating those." Gabbie yelped and managed to kick him in the shin, but he nabbed the box and escaped with it to his room. He locked the door and stripped down to his boxers and climbed under his NASCAR quilt. He took some of his polished rocks and put them under the quilt with him. He put a pile of them on his stomach. They were as cold as ice cubes and about as comforting, but the feel of them on his bare skin gave him a rush. This was what it was to be almost through puberty and not even twelve years old—to be eating crackers in bed and getting off on frozen rocks. He had one repeating thought like an abusive mantra: I'm nearly twelve years old and what have I accomplished? Nothing. What if nothing in his life ever worked out? What if every business idea of his failed as spectacularly as the rock selling experiment? He would end up like Dale, dressed in an oversized Zellers track suit, giving away bags of frozen food to desperate young boys who didn't want raw, frozen crinkle cuts, but felt too sorry for him or afraid of him to say no. Still, the cold feel of the frozen rocks as Nathan moved them around his body made his own skin feel like it belonged to him in a way for which he had no words.

In the weeks and months following Lynette's revelation, Jack tried hate, rage and confrontation, but all roads led to distraction. Watching Lynette's blossoming body and maniacal good mood, he couldn't maintain his hostility. Instead of making plans for war or divorce, Jack was off in a corner of the library reading in a journal about how Thomas Carlyle loaned his manuscript of *The French Revolution* to his dear friend John Stuart Mill. Somehow, Mill inadvertently burned the manuscript to ashes. When he came to tell his friend about it, Carlyle was gracious, comforting, and even praised Mill for his forthright approach. Carlyle's manuscript was lost forever. Even if he rewrote it, which he eventually did, it could never be the same. Still, it was Carlyle who consoled Mill when Mill broke the incomprehensible news about the inexplicably destroyed pages. It was only later, because of the slavery issue, that Mill decided to despise Carlyle and end the friendship. How, Jack wondered, could you judge and condemn someone who had been so saintly in his understanding of you, even if his views were beyond despicable? Did Mill really believe that compassion was something to be carefully meted out to the deserving and haughtily withheld from the wretched?

Jack was uncomfortable with Lynette's Christian zeal but he wanted to believe in Christian love and forgiveness as a force for good in the world. This all made sense in the library and almost made sense at home where Nathan, lonely and vengeful, took out his pains on delightful, victimized Gabbie and Lynette sang gospel songs louder and louder to drown everyone out. He would try to make it make sense.

While Lynette sang from the kitchen, Gabbie sat on Jack's lap and he read to her the story "The Little Match Girl" from Hans Christian Andersen. She cried and asked if the little girl really got to be with her grandmother again after the last match burned up. "Of course," he said, even though the image of the little girl frozen on the steps outside the happy family's home was always more vivid to him than her ethereal reunion with the kind grandmother, who was dead before the story even began.

Gabbie was a wriggler by nature and barely lasted to the end of the brief story, but it felt good to sit with her for those few minutes. To distract her from her sorrow over "The Little Match Girl," he asked her what she would do if someone took something she had written, a story, or a picture she had made, and accidentally threw it into a fire. "If Nathan did that to me, I'd take the burning ashes and put them into his bed with him when he was sleeping," she answered dreamily. "I love you, Daddy," she added, putting her arms around his neck. Her hair smelled like artificial bananas from the No More Tangles/No More Tears shampoo. Jack hugged her back until she squirmed herself free from his lap. She floated off to find out what was for supper.

Lynette was making tuna casserole, the kind with canned mushroom soup, frozen peas and those crunchy chow mein noodles. It was the best supper to prepare because it was fail-safe and everyone would eat it. She let Gabbie open the cans of tuna and soup and steal a few noodles. Instead of salad, she cut up carrots and celery and cucumbers so everyone could take their pick. Nathan sauntered through the kitchen. When his mom told him there was tuna casserole in the oven and he saw her letting Gabbie stir the chocolate pudding they were making, he wondered what the payback for this meal would be. Was this his last meal before they sent him to boarding school? Was his third cousin Ricky, the soccer player and insufferable braggart, coming for an extended visit?

When he was younger, Nathan had been obsessed with superheroes, then airplanes, and now corporate success. These fantasies all grew out of the aftermath of the joyous anticipation of family meals such as this one. When Nathan grew up, he would be far too busy and successful to sit through such meals. Nathan would be the kind of executive who would send life-sized stuffed pandas perched on the shoulders of singing telegram delivery boys to his kids on their birthdays. All the while, important work would keep him zooming through the skies in his private jet. He would unfasten his seat belt, sip a colourful, sweetened drink, and take a few seconds to imagine his children's cries of joy as they received their gifts.

They sat down to eat at the pine table in the kitchen nook. Nathan served himself while Gabbie said grace. She and

Nathan sat across from each other, facing off over the cucumber slices. Lynette hadn't told the kids about the baby. Well, not directly. She was pretty sure they knew, though, and thought they must be happy about it. There was barely room for her belly when she squeezed onto the bench, so they had to know.

"Okay, guys. We need to talk."

"Here we go." Nathan put his head down and ate like he was a vacuum cleaner.

Gabbie, who was a nibbler, swirled her noodles and peas around on her plate and sang a jingle from a commercial for *My Little Pony* to herself.

"Jack, Honey—you tell them," Lynette said, smiling at him. "Tell them the wonderful news."

Jack's fury had dampened in the months since he'd tried to adjust to the news, but he wasn't prepared to be the lighthearted messenger for Nathan and Gabbie. "Hey, kids, your mother and I are getting a divorce," Jack said, grinning like he was making a hilarious joke. "But you know we both still love you."

Gabbie smashed her glass of milk down on the table, spilling most of it. "I'm staying with Mommy," she blurted.

At the same time, Nathan said, "Hallelujah, it's about time."

"Oh, Daddy, you're such a kidder," Lynette said. "But that's not the way to talk at the table. Tell them, Honey. Tell them."

"We've been blessed," Jack said. "For a third time. There's going to be one more little Grunberg in the world."

Gabbie asked, "Are you really getting a divorce?"

"Of course not, you stupid freak. Dad just said that so we'd be happy about the real news," Nathan said.

"You really are getting a baby brother or sister," Lynette

said, "and you're going to love that little baby so much and she's going to love you even more."

"It's a girl?" Gabbie asked.

"We don't know that yet, Sweetheart, but whatever it is will be fine."

"Aren't you kind of old to have a baby, Mom?" Nathan asked. "What if it's got like two heads or eighteen toes because your eggs are stale?"

"Nathan! Your mother's eggs are not stale," Jack said in his stern fatherly voice. "You don't ever speak that way about your mother."

"It has to be a girl," Gabbie said, "or it'll be a psycho like Nathan. I can't live in a house with two Nathans. I'll kill myself."

"Freak-Baby-Two-Heads will put its brains together and help you off yourself," Nathan said.

"And there's more," Lynette said, easing herself up from the bench. "We're going to have a home birth. I've got a midwife and my friend Ann-Marie is going to be my doula, so we're all going to be here together to be part of the miracle of life."

"Is this the part where you say you're kidding and you and Dad really are getting a divorce?" Nathan asked. "Because that might be a good idea. There is no way Dad is going to make it through any home birth and there is no way I'm going anywhere near that."

The home birth part was news to Jack but he was beyond reacting. What good would it do? He jumped up and started doing laps around the imaginary track that ran through the kitchen, living room and dining room. Lynette started cleaning up the dinner dishes and the kids retreated to the television. Lynette took the pudding out of the fridge and divided it into four bowls. She took the can of whipping cream and sprayed a dollop on each bowl. For Gabbie, she added multi-coloured sprinkles. "Kids. Jack, come have dessert," Lynette called out.

Nathan would be the photographer. He had a Polaroid camera and Mom had promised him two whole rolls of film: one for the birth and one for Nathan to use for whatever he wanted. Nathan loved the camera but the film was expensive and whenever there was any, there were endless negotiations, in the form of shrieking, threatening, sobbing and storming off, over who got to take which shots. Nathan had once been grounded for a whole weekend except for Sunday school because he wasted a precious shot on the rotting contents of the refrigerator's vegetable drawer. So Nathan was up for the bribe to be the birth photographer. "But I'm only doing before and after shots," he said. "Nothing of it actually coming out."

"Nathan, Honey. Birth is so natural. When you're there and it's really happening, you won't be frightened, just amazed," Lynette told him.

"I'm not afraid, just grossed out," Nathan said.

Gabbie wanted to be the flower girl and held on to this notion, despite the abuse Nathan heaped on her for even suggesting it.

"Flabby Gabbie thinks she's going to a wedding," he said first and then, whenever she said anything or even didn't say anything, he would look at her with pseudo-love in his eyes and say, "You may now kiss the bride of Frankenstein."

In the end she compromised on a new dress—green velour with a lace collar and a ribbon sash—which was a miracle find for Lynette at Zellers, where it is hard to find anything except acrylic Christmas sweaters and half-price fondue sets. "It will be kind of a birthday party, Gabbie," Lynette told her. "You can dress up and get everyone refreshments."

Jack wanted to disappear in a rabbit hole and emerge in Wonderland—some kind of place where language rules, not incontrovertible facts, and where sounds, not meanings, are truths; most of all, a place where no one has to act like a grown-up and where everyone's childishness is taken seriously.

As the day grew closer, Lynette felt everything had been arranged by God. When the first mild contractions started around five in the morning, she lay in bed for a while with her hands on her belly and prayed her gratitude. She asked for nothing in her prayer, only gave thanks. This attitude of prayer was something she had worked for years to get to, and was only now finding it came easily and joyously. The baby was too big to move much inside her, but sometimes she felt a jab from a fist or foot against her that was stronger than a tickle but didn't quite hurt. She felt happy and unafraid. No one under the age of thirty-five should give birth, she thought. They are too scared, too selfish and too weak. Maybe no one who hasn't done it before should give birth. It was knowing that she had survived Nathan's difficult birth and Gabbie's surprisingly easy birth that made Lynette so breezy and delighted about this one.

The third time Lynette woke up to pee, she saw a bloody, yellow glob of something in the toilet bowl and realized that her mucus plug had broken loose. It was like the moment when the pregnancy test showed what she already knew. There is no turning back, she thought, and simultaneously recognized what an absurd thought it was. Pregnancy and childbirth are not like riding a train, they are like being a train. When Lynette stood up, the next contraction hit a little harder. She leaned into the door frame so she wouldn't keel over or yelp. When it was over, she came back to the bed and stood next to Jack's side.

"Jack," she whispered. "Jack."

"What time is it?"

Instead of answering, she sang a little bit of "Bound for Glory," the song about the train they both loved and that Jack used to sing for her when she was young and terrified and pregnant with Nathan.

Sierra

They were having this party and Gabbie's mom was rolling around on the bed, which had been pushed into the centre of the living room, in her nightgown, groaning like a wounded cow. Gabbie had her new green dress on and there were guests but they were all there to help Gabbie's mom have this baby. Nathan wouldn't take a picture of Gabbie in her dress. He just wouldn't. The guests were three women who drove up in a big, rusty, red station wagon and parked it sideways right across the driveway. The women, Ann-Marie, Eva and Marnie, were right away taking over the house, busy with sheets and massage oils and stethoscopes and candles. They looked like three witches with their long, frizzy grey hair, their long cotton dresses and their big scary grins. Marnie was the midwife. She had the power to get the baby out. Ann-Marie, the doula, was like Cinderella. Her job was to do everything for Lynette and the other women.

Eva was the assistant midwife. She was learning to get babies out but she had a wandering eye and funny teeth and a miniature old man's beer belly. Gabbie doubted she had the magical power to make a baby come out.

They were all nice to Gabbie in the way her mom was when she came home with the new dress. Nice because they're so wackin' happy all the time because they eat right and dress in bright colours. Or maybe, Gabbie thought, nice because they have set you up for some big trick, like when Erika Findlayson said Gabbie could go over to her house after school and smiled at her all day like that until the bell rang and then, when Gabbie bounded up to Erika and Samantha, Erika said Samantha had paid her a dollar just to say that and who did Gabbie think she was? That she was some kind of special princess that Erika would ever, she meant ever, invite Gabbie to her house? And then Erika and Samantha walked home together, holding hands and skipping and smiling like that and the other girls skipped after them, a few paces behind because they weren't allowed to go to Erika's that afternoon, but close enough to them and far enough away from Gabbie that it showed that they knew that some day soon they would get their invite to Erika's, and that Gabbie would get hers when hell froze over. That happened to Gabbie in grade one and even though Erika had moved away in grade two and Samantha was a nobody without her and had to hang around with Alicia McNickers who spent half of every day in Special Ed and Gabbie had since made her own girl clique with Jen and Jessica, she never forgot it. Whenever her friends were too kind to her, she wondered what they were plotting.

Marnie and Eva and Ann-Marie smiled at Gabbie in that nicey-nice way and talked to her like they knew her really well. "Gabbie, would you like to rub your mother's back for us, Honey?" "Gabbie, do you know how to make a pitcher of lemonade or do you need help with that?"

Gabbie looked at Lynette, all heaving and twisting on the mattress and she thought, this baby's going to kill her. That's for sure. And I will have to live with Dad, which would be okay, but he's never around even when he is around. Like now. He was to be part of the birth party, but we don't know where he is. We are all in the living room with the mattress in the middle of the room but Dad is who knows where. He is hiding out somewhere like he always did.

Gabbie asked Ann-Marie if Mom was dying. She said no and that Gabbie should put on Mom's favourite tape, so she put on that Nina Simone one about how Nina Simone's dad was a miner, but now she lives in Paris where her children get to dance and have a good life. It was such a pretty song and Gabbie danced to it for her mom, but Lynette kept making beached beluga noises and Nathan looked completely freaked. He had lost his usual ability to say something mean in every breath. He was pacing around like Jack. He took it upon himself to be as wound up and as helpless as Jack would have been if he had shown his face.

It was best when Lynette was incoherent. During contractions she swore and squealed and cried. In between the contractions she said things like, "Honey, isn't this the most amazing thing?" and "Praise the Lord, children. We're making a miracle, right here in this house."

This went on until nighttime, when one of the women made this lentil and fennel soup that Gabbie figured they made for every birth. It reeked and if Nathan weren't freaking he would have said they made it to smoke the baby out of its hole. The women ate the soup. They raved about how delicious it was. Apparently it was the best lentil and fennel soup in the history of childbirth. Nathan and Gabbie ate white bread with marshmallow spread on it. The women smiled sadly at the little streaks of marshmallow goo on Gabbie's and Nathan's faces. Their children loved lentil and fennel soup, they all said. It was a treat for them like ice cream or licorice. Gabbie and Nathan would probably love it too if they only tried it. "No thanks," the children said. "We're allergic," Gabbie said. The women grinned all the more at Gabbie's lie but didn't challenge her.

The labour went on forever. Nathan took a picture of the remains of the soup—evidence, he said. Finally, even the gnawing terror that their mom was dying and Gabbie and Nathan were going to be orphans like kids in an adventure movie and the looking away from Mom writhing there like an animal on the mattress on the living room floor were boring. The women kept telling Lynette to get up and walk around or to take a bath or something, but she wouldn't budge. It felt too right, she told them. By this time, Gabbie and Nathan had both fallen asleep on the sofa, Gabbie curled up in a ball the size of a large cat next to Nathan, who was stretched out already, taking up most of the space.

"Jack," Marnie said, "we need to talk this over with you and Lynette together." It had been twenty hours of Lynette on the bed in the living room. Jack had floated through most of it, but now they were reeling him in. "Jack, she's barely dilated and we're concerned about the heartbeat. We would like to give it some more time, but we want you to be part of this decision."

If Jack hadn't been so tired, he would have laughed. Now they wanted his opinion. "Look, ladies. I'm not a midwife and I'm not a doctor."

At this point, Lynette had another contraction and resumed bellowing. The three women sprang into action around her, massaging her, holding her hand, breathing with her. When she could speak, Lynette said in a barely audible whisper, "I want it out of me now. I want it out."

"Shhh. Shhh," the women said. They are nurturing, Jack thought, but they are not really witches and they have no magic to draw on to turn this nightmare into the miracle Lynette needs.

"You heard the lady," Jack said. "Get it out now."

Marnie asked for quiet so she could record the baby's heartbeat. "Quiet, I can't hear it," she said, and everyone froze, waiting for her to say, yes, it's fine. "I can't hear it," she said again.

Jack was about to say, Lynette, Honey, maybe we should go into the hospital, just in case, but the midwives beat him to it. Marnie called the hospital while Ann-Marie and Eva tried to get Lynette ready to go. They helped her dress between writhing through contractions. The one with the freaky eye, Eva, offered to stay home with Nathan and Gabbie. Everyone else bundled into the station wagon, Jack in the back seat next to Lynette who was in a blanket, doubling over again in another contraction. Ann-Marie cranked the key and the engine almost caught, but it wouldn't. Jack looked and saw that the old guzzler was out of gas.

"Holy fucking shit, what is this?" he wanted to demand like an irate customer at an overpriced restaurant, but he was not a driver (never had a licence) and he was also not a midwife or a doctor. He was depending on these women to save his wife's and baby's lives. Now didn't seem the time to get into it with them. Ann-Marie and Lynette had a good laugh over the car's being out of gas when they finally realized what the problem was. "Take my car," Lynette said. But the station wagon was parked sideways across the driveway and had completely blocked off the garage where the car was. The station wagon was not going anywhere any time soon.

Marnie ran back into the house to call an ambulance. The hospital people argued about the ambulance. "Are you sure this is an emergency?" they asked. Women in labour apparently call all the time demanding ambulances and tying up the system when they should know there is plenty of time. Gabbie, who was sleeping on the couch nearby, woke up enough to hear something she didn't understand: "foetal distress"—and then something she did: "Do you want a dead baby and a dead mother on your hands?"

At the hospital, there were no candles, no soft music and no laughing party atmosphere. Lynette was strapped on a gurney and whisked away by a fat orderly with greasy pores. Ann-Marie and Marnie fought to stick around, but were treated as persona non grata by the hospital types. "Are you related to the patient?" they wanted to know. "If not, you can wait in the waiting room." Jack was told to fill out forms. "I want my women with me," Lynette pleaded. Ann-Marie was crying. Marnie said it was a mistake to come here; that nothing good could come of it.

As Jack made his way down the hall to find Lynette, Ann-Marie and Marnie walked him to the threshold, whispering advice, consoling him as though there had been a terrible tragedy; as though there was no hope for the baby or Lynette now that the hospital was in charge. "Don't let them use the internal monitor," they said. "It hurts the baby." "If you can just help her relax and stall them on the C-section thing, I think she still can do this naturally."

Jack pushed past them, saying, "Thanks so much." Not

until months later did he realize that this was the point where he could have told both of them to take a flying leap. He made his way into Lynette's room. She was on a thin hospital bed with various IVs, still writhing and still begging for Ann-Marie. Jack was asked to leave while the anesthesiologist came in to do the epidural.

In the hallway, a nurse with watery, red eyes and a button on her uniform that said "I ❤ Breast Feeding" explained that the epidural would mean Lynette was ready to go straight to the emergency C-section if she needed it, but they'd found the heartbeat now. "It was steady."

Jack nodded, trying to look as though he was relieved they weren't going directly to surgery but thinking now it really would go on forever. He wanted to like these medical people more than the midwives, to trust them and believe that they had the power over life and death. The hospital types thought he was one of these granola types and wanted to convince him that they loved letting nature take its course, that they weren't hardcore interventionists. "Just get the baby out," he told the runny-eyed nurse. "Process is overrated."

The nurse looked at him harshly, though her weepy eyes made her look compassionate too. "Maybe," she said, "but without the luxury of time travel, you have to be present here to go through the process of getting you and your wife and your baby through this."

She was telling Jack that none of his hiding places, in books, in the rec room, in his head, at work, would shield him here. He had to look back at this nurse and he wondered briefly whether she starched her uniform. He wondered if she would talk so convincingly if her uniform were grey or rumpled or had mustard stains on it.

"Okay," he said. "Let's get through this."

The nurse smiled at him and gripped his arm as if she were his third grade teacher and he had just made her very proud. He stood close to the door to Lynette's room and listened. Lynette was screaming, really out of control now, and the anesthesiologist was saying, "Now be still. Don't move! Or the needle will break off in your back."

The pain of this labour was nothing like the other two. They say you forget the pain, but Lynette remembered it now and this one was a hundred times worse. It was worse than a root canal without anesthetic. The other two labours were more like the awful intensity of bad migraines, except you got breaks between the contractions. A migraine is worse because there are no breaks. The pain of this one was inhuman. Lynette could only think this through once she'd had the epidural, which made her feel like the blood in the lower half of her body was too warm. She felt woozy, then nauseous, then blessedly numb. Jack held her hand and told her not to give up. He wanted her to have the C-section, she knew, he wanted to punish her for foisting this whole home birth thing on him, well this whole birth thing, really, but she didn't care any more. She just wanted out. She could have been sad and humiliated about not being woman enough to squat in a field and have a baby like tribal woman supposedly did, or she could have raged against the hospital for shoving her full of IVs and making her midwife and her doula stay in the emergency waiting room with the knife-fight victims and the asthmatic kids. Luckily, none of it mattered.

Jack kept saying, "You're doing so great. Just a little longer." What did he want? Some kind of father of the year award?

When they screwed the heart rate monitor right into her baby, Lynnette had stopped caring. They reached inside her body and did that to her baby's head. To hell with what Marnie said about fighting them on that. Lynette felt like maybe she wasn't here any more. Maybe this was what death felt like. What a surprise—no peace, no eternal bliss or eternal nothingness; no nestling in Jesus's arms, only endless present-tense agony. Maybe she was in hell right here and now. This was her punishment for having this baby without Jack's blessing. But even in hell, there are some benefits. If you're already damned, at least you can quit trying.

Lynette whistled as the doctor tried to explain the pros and cons of waiting a little longer versus going straight to surgery. She was six centimetres dilated now, not really progressing as he would like; maybe she was just too worn out; childbirth is harder when you're over thirty-five. If she wanted him to open her up right now and get the baby out, he would do it. If she wanted to wait, he was willing to give her another few hours—tops—and then she might be facing the C-section anyway. "I don't want either," she said. "I don't want any of this." Jack paced around, trying to stay out of it. She knew what he wanted: he loved the idea of surgery and doctors fixing everything, so long as he wasn't the one under the knife.

Finally the doctor said, "Well, then. We'll give it some time. You two discuss it," and he left the room.

In the end, the baby made the decision. When the doctor came back in to see what Jack and Lynette wanted to do, the baby's head was crowning. With the epidural, Lynette hadn't even felt the change. She delivered little Sierra in about three pushes. It was surreal, Jack thought. With the other two kids, the final stage of labour, pushing the baby out, had been the most horrific. Jack, who had been plea bargaining with God, offering up every single one of his vices for an outcome just like this, was ecstatic and relieved. He immediately renegotiated his promise to read less. No benign God could hold him to a promise made under such dire circumstances.

Jack cut the cord and the nurse wrapped the baby up and gave her to Lynette. Sierra was red and scrawny with a little tuft of black hair. Lynette looked at her and said, "It looks like a little alien."

Sierra had a scrape on the top of her head where they had screwed in the monitor. Lynette looked at the red and purple spot on Sierra's head. Her baby was less than five minutes old and already she was damaged.

"My, she's a beauty," the nurse said.

The baby's head had a kind of wedge shape to it and its eyes were crusty and shut.

Lynette looked at Sierra, red, waxy, wrinkled and fervently exhausted, and thought this baby was not the one she'd been expecting. This was some other, crappier, everyday baby, not her miracle child at all. Everyone said nice things and Jack's eyes were all misty. Lynette knew she had to pretend even harder than everyone else that the baby was fine. She tried to make a joke out of how freakish the baby looked. She said, "Beam her up, Scotty. This one's coming home."

Gabbie woke up and stretched, She stayed quiet until Eva thought she was asleep and retreated to the kitchen. Then Gabbie pinched Nathan awake. "Nathan! Nathan! Right now," she said in their mother's you're-going-to-be-late-for-school-if-you-don't-get-up-this-instant voice.

Nathan sat up and looked at her.

"Shhhh," she said. "Mom's dead. They took her to the hospital to die and left us here with that Eva."

"How do you know?"

"I heard them talking. They thought I was asleep."

Nathan was now fully awake. For some reason, this was the first moment in his life when he didn't doubt his sister. He had known all along how this would come out. "What about the baby?"

"Dead, I think," Gabbie said, twirling a long strand of her hair around and around her finger.

"Good," Nathan said. "Or else I'd kill it myself." Finally, Gabbie and Nathan had a reason for a truce: a common enemy. They both understood that this unexpected, unnecessary baby had killed their mother.

"I'd drown it," said Gabbie.

"I'd wring its neck."

"I'd punt it."

"Put a pillow over its face."

"Leave it out in the snow."

"Poison it."

"Wallop it."

They sat together on the couch, close to each other but not touching, remembering times with Mom when she was looking after them all the time. They tried to think about growing up from now on without her, but they couldn't. They just hit a wall. They both imagined, in spite of themselves, Mom and Dad coming home from the hospital with the new baby and everything being as it was. Then they imagined putting time into reverse to a few days ago or to months ago, before the tuna casserole dinner when Mom told them about the baby, but there was no way to stop thinking and no thought that was safe to dwell on. Gabbie said, "Nathan, when you grow up and you have your jet, can I fly on it with you?"

Nathan said, "Maybe. If I'm not on important business. Probably you could."

The phone rang and they started as if they had been zapped with an electric prod. Eva answered it. They heard her in the kitchen saying, "Really? Really? Praise be to Jesus."

They didn't want to know, but they also had to know, so they went into the kitchen and asked Eva.

"Everything is fine," Eva said. "Your mother and the baby are fine. She didn't have a C-section, and your mama and your new baby sister are just fine."

"They're not dead?"

"Of course not, Sweetie. Your daddy's on his way home now and Mom and the baby are coming home tomorrow. If everyone isn't too tired, maybe you kids can go meet your new sister tonight."

They waited up for Jack and when the taxi pulled in, they ran to meet him. The three of them hugged each other and cried and Gabbie kept making Jack say it over and over again: "Mother and baby are recovering well."

Acknowledgements

I would like to thank George Toles and Mary Schendlinger for their careful reading of numerous drafts and for using love and patience and gentle honesty to help me to make the stories better. Thanks to my parents and siblings for their faith in me. Thanks to the Toles family for their warm embrace and especially Rose Toles for her courageous and compassionate example. Thanks to Annabel, Brenda, Jenny, Kim, Miriam, Shaunna and Sue for the walks, talks, sushi and laughs. Thanks also to everyone at Turnstone for saying yes and staying with me and to Paul and Holly McNally for all their support. Thanks also to the Manitoba Arts Council.